THE SOLID GOLD KID

"You are all, with the exception of Derek, here by chance. Unlucky for you. We didn't ask you to get into the van, but once you did, you were stuck. There's no way in the world that you can get away till we have what we're here for. You understand?

"Derek is our prize, our little gold nugget. Our solid gold kid. The rest of you aren't worth two cents. . . ."

Other Bantam Starfire Books you will enjoy

THE SOLID GOLD KID

A Novel by

NORMA FOX MAZER

and

HARRY MAZER

BANTAM BOOKS
NEW YORK • TORONTO • LONDON • SYDNEY • AUCKLAND

RL5, IL age 12 and up

THE SOLID GOLD KID

*A Bantam Book / published by arrangement with
the author*

PRINTING HISTORY

Original hardcover edition published 1977

*The Starfire logo is a registered trademark of Bantam Books,
a division of Bantam Doubleday Dell Publishing Group, Inc.
Registered in U.S. Patent and Trademark Office and elsewhere*

Bantam edition / April 1989

ISBN 0-553-27851-7

Published simultaneously in the United States and Canada

---

*Bantam Books are published by Bantam Books, a division of Bantam Doubleday
Dell Publishing Group, Inc. Its trademark, consisting of the words "Bantam
Books" and the portrayal of a rooster, is Registered in U.S. Patent and
Trademark Office and in other countries. Marca Registrada. Bantam Books,
666 Fifth Avenue, New York, New York 10103.*

PRINTED IN THE UNITED STATES OF AMERICA

KR   0 9 8 7 6 5 4 3 2 1

1

That particular Saturday in April it was raining. It had been raining hard all night, and though it had let up some, it continued into the morning. I thought about not going downtown as I usually did, but what was I going to do hanging around school? Every Saturday for months I'd been going into the city to Simon's Place, a dark, smoky barn on Second Street, to hear bluegrass groups.

I'm crazy about bluegrass. It's been springing up around here and all over the country the last few years. I don't play any instrument myself—well, I have taken piano lessons and so forth, but that doesn't count. What I am, as far as music goes, is a listener. I really admire those musicians who get up there on the stage at Simon's and play. They have skill and nerve, both of which I feel deficient in. I've wondered how they found out they wanted to be musicians. Though I think about it a lot, I don't know what I want to be. I just seem to be coasting along, enjoying life as it comes.

Weekends, half of Payne School goes home—I do, too, if Dad happens to be in the city. Marcia, Dad's secretary, usually calls the school and leaves a message for me if Dad is around, and I'll hop a plane to Kennedy on Friday night and either take a taxi into the city or else find the car waiting with Mac, Dad's chauffeur, behind the wheel. "How are you, Derek?" he always says. "Nice to see you." And that's that. Mac George has been Dad's chauffeur for about the last five years, but I have yet to have more than a three-sentence conversation with him.

I get to see Dad about once every three months if I'm lucky. Most weekends, though, I'm right here on campus. And almost every Saturday I take the 12:22 Common Center bus that stops on Payne Road down beyond the main gates, and I go to Simon's to hear bluegrass groups like the Henry David Thoreau Memorial Band and the Dishwater Blues Band.

That morning I was in my room, lying on the bed and bouncing a tennis ball off the ceiling. "Come on, Chapman, how about it? Put your shoulder to the wheel." My roommate, Noah Greenwood, had that anxious Saturday-morning-inspection look in his eyes. I could hardly remember all the roommates I'd had over the last eight years. I'd been making the boarding school–prep school rounds ever since my parents split. My mom took my sister, Ora, and moved to Laguna Beach, California, and Dad and I moved into the penthouse on Central Park South in New York City.

Dad has a genius for sending me to bum boarding

schools where, invariably, I am the resident really-rich-kid. Not that Payne School was exactly overflowing with the poor and downtrodden, but their fathers were mostly doctors and company-executive types, while mine is Jimmy Neal Chapman.

My father started making money when he was still in high school by manufacturing and selling his own pharmaceuticals from my grandmother's basement in the East Bronx. By the time he was nineteen he'd sold that business and had his first million. If you read any of the articles about Dad, you'll see they always use words like "cunning" and "self-made" and "opportune moments" (which the writers always say he's seizing).

Dad says the world is suspicious of anyone who's made money as fast as he has by his wits and guts, but if you've inherited from your grandfather (who probably made *his* money by his wits and guts) all you get is respect. It might have been different (for me, I mean) if we'd been old money, and I'd grown up with Rockefellers, Whitneys, and Lodges. I would have been sent to all the "right" schools and not stood out like a sore thumb. And maybe I'd be aware of my *social responsibilities* and what I should contribute to my school and my country. I mean, can you imagine Nelson R. wasting his morning bouncing tennis balls off a ceiling? And, at the advanced age of sixteen, brooding over what he's doing here in the world and why he's never had a real, very close, friend?

"Maybe I shouldn't go downtown." Rain splashed down the outside of the windows.

"Maybe you better get your ass in motion," Greenie said. "The Room Committee is on the floor already. It's not that hard a room to clean," he added.

"Right," I said, glancing over to his side of the room, which was at least five hundred percent cleaner than mine. Payne School believed in cold showers, iron beds, and oatmeal for breakfast. As Hiram Putney Payne, Our Founder, said one hundred ten years ago, "Neatness, restraint, and self-discipline are the first steps in encouraging Youth to lead Useful and Productive lives."

I looked around at the clock on the bureau. "You sure that time is right?" If I missed the 12:22 bus I'd either have to wait two hours or hoof it into the city.

"You still have time," Greenie said. "You don't want another demerit, do you, Chapman?"

"Greenie," I said, getting to my feet, "you're a true and loyal son of Payne School." I shoved the mess on my desk into a drawer and scuffed together a few floating dust balls with my sneaker. Greenie was piling stuff on top of my bed: battered copies of *Harvard Lampoon,* a clutch of orange tennis balls, an American-history review book, and a peach that had been attacked by a deadly green fungus.

"These are yours, Chapman. Better hop to it, I hear them!"

I dropped the tennis balls, the peach, and the magazines into the wastebasket. The overflow I threw into the closet. "Don't you ever put your mind on higher things, Greenie? Is your whole aim in life to have a clean room to show the Room Committee?"

"You better make your bed with hospital corners, and don't forget your wastebasket and the closet."

I took a few more swipes at my side of the room. I just couldn't get passionate about it.

"On your toes, Chapman. They're coming."

I could hear Will Harmon, Chairman of the Room Committee, snapping them to attention next door. He and I had had it out the night before—at least he had it out, and I had it. He'd caught up to me on the Quad. "Hold it there, Chapman! Hold it right there. I've just come from a meeting of the Payne Club executive board. You've turned down the best club in school. Why? Can you tell me why? Never mind, I'll tell you why. Pure, unadulterated snobbery!"

"I disagree," I said.

"All the brothers think so, Chapman." He started in with that phony fraternity fellowship crap. "We've all seen you with that know-it-all look on your face. You hold yourself aloof, Chapman. We're all regular fellows, but you seem to think you're a special breed of human being." He grabbed my shirt. "Stop jumping around like a grasshopper, and listen to me!"

I jerked away and buttoned up my jacket, then unbuttoned it.

"What's the matter, Chapman, can't stand the plebeian touch?" I noticed his hands, all knuckles and soapy pink. He was just aching for me to make a move. I stuck my hands in my pockets. I have this thing about violence. I don't believe fighting ever settles anything. I'm nonviolent by choice. The only trouble with being nonviolent is that you find yourself worrying what if you're really just basically a coward? If you're feeling a little down, you can make yourself feel really punky thinking that way. But still I would rather walk away from a fight than be put in the position of punching or hurting someone else. Only one time in my life have I hated anyone enough to want to hurt them physically, violently. And then, it couldn't change what had already happened.

Now, hearing Harmon's voice again, I pulled on my tweed jacket. It was time to leave. Nothing was going to convince Will Harmon that I'd turned down Payne Club just because I didn't want to be a snob and a phony. I'd never shown any interest in Payne Club, so why had they asked me to join? It could only be the charm of the Chapman millions. Not one of those guys was, ever had been, or ever meant to be my friend.

Outside the rain was coming down hard again. The sky was gray. Lights were on in most of the buildings. I had ten or fifteen minutes to kill before my bus, so I ducked into Chapman Hall to wait. It's a big new auditorium–lecture center, and because Dad donated a big hunk of money he got his name on it. His picture, too, top-lighted, hanging smack in the middle of the front wall as you enter—one of those Chairman-of-the-Board portraits with Dad in a blue silk business suit, one hand in his jacket pocket and the other gesturing. The artist made Dad look taller, smoother, better looking, sort of golden. The fact is Dad is short and dark, with shoulders like a football player. Once, when Mom and Dad were still together, a newspaper article described them as Beauty and the Beast, which is an exaggeration but sort of true. My mother is three inches taller than Dad, one of those thin Swedish blonds and really beautiful. I'm a combination, dark like Dad but tall like Mom.

My parents are really the original mismatched couple. Dad's always on the move. He has so much energy he can't hold still for a minute. I fidget like him, too, only I'm not going anywhere. He hardly stops to sleep. He uses our New York apartment (with all those white rugs some decorator did to us) like one of his hotel stops. I've seen him stay up all night with work, then take a twenty-minute nap on the couch and wake up raring to go. Mom couldn't take that. She's really a very private person.

"Business good?" I said, glancing up at Dad's portrait. The overhead light cast a glow over the canvas. "Can't say the same for me. Remember, Dad, I said something about it the last time we got together? You thought I was being sensitive, but they take themselves too tight-assed serious here, Dad."

New Year's Day he and I had driven up to Pelham Bay on Long Island Sound. Mostly Mac drives him in the Bentley, so he can work while he's going someplace. But for fun Dad has a little silver sports Mercedes, a 300 SL.

That's what we took that day. We skimmed stones across the water and then we ran the whole length of the frozen beach to the bridge and crossed over to City Island. There wasn't a soul around. Just the birds and us. We ate fish chowder at a diner, and Dad talked about buying a house overlooking the ocean. But later he said it wasn't practical with both of us away most of the year. Christmas vacation was the only time we were even halfway sure of being together for a few days.

Applause broke into my communing with Dad. The double doors of Lecture Hall A were pushed open from inside. I glanced in. A man was standing at the podium. ". . . be glad now to answer any questions," he was saying. "Those of you that have to leave, feel free to do so." A handful of kids trailed out—all townies. The girl who came out first, carrying a notebook, caught my eye. There was something arresting about her, maybe the way she walked—fast, her back straight, but with this calm, self-contained expression. She had a thick, ropy blond braid hanging over one shoulder, and exquisite ears with tiny little gold hoops. I always look at ears. Is that a weird thing to notice in girls?

I like girls. I like my sister, Ora. I like my mother. I'm not shy, but I've never been a dazzling success with any girl. Two summers ago, at a tennis camp in the Poconos, there was a girl, Gene. Eugenia Ellis. She loved to sing, knew dozens of songs. She had a tiny, tiny waist and round breasts, a fantastic body. I wanted to look at her breasts all the time, touch them, but that just made her mad. *Aren't you ever serious, Derek? It's because you're rich.* She was rich, too, though not rich like us.

One night, after the big Camp Wa-Ken-Eh bonfire and songfest, we were alone at the edge of the playing field. Gene made me sit on the benches while she undressed completely and let me look at her so we could get it over with and get back to more important things. Maybe I'm not aggressive enough. I know I'm not.

I followed the blond girl out of the hall, out into the rain. She pulled up the collar of her yellow slicker. I wasn't wearing a raincoat, so the rain plastered my hair and ran down my neck.

In a moment I was going to speak to her, introduce myself, find out her name. We were going to be friends. My mind leaped ahead to the questions I'd ask her about herself, to the long conversations we'd have. What would I say first? Nothing stupid like "I saw you in the lecture hall." My first words couldn't be ordinary.

All at once the girl turned and glanced at me. I half raised my hand. Her eyebrows went up—thick dark eyebrows with all that blond hair. It was the perfect moment to speak, but I couldn't say a word.

On Payne Road she stopped by the white-and-blue bus sign at the corner beyond the main gates. What luck! In a few minutes we'd be on the same bus together. A few other kids who'd come out of the lecture hall were waiting there too, all of us in the rain. A tall, cocky-looking Black guy in a white knit sweater leaned against the bus sign with his arms crossed. He was almost too good-looking. A little fat around the middle, though.

"Hey!" he said to me. "Know when the bus comes?"

"A few minutes," I answered, watching the blond girl.

"We'll drown if it doesn't come fast," said a girl sheltering a tiny poodle in her arms. With a green kerchief on her head (wiry red hair sticking out all over), she looked something like Little Orphan Annie. She was wearing a green button-down sweater, and there was a green canvas bag at her feet.

I stood next to the blond girl. "The bus will be here soon," I said to her. Brilliant opening! She gave me that lifted-eyebrows look again.

"How soon?" she asked. I thought her voice was beautiful, low and smooth.

"About ten more minutes." Another fantastic Chapman conversational gambit! Anyway, it was working. Sort of.

"Really? Ten minutes?"

"Yes." I looked down at my wristwatch. "Well, actually, it's more like eight minutes." Everything I said to her was about the time. What could be more ordinary and dull? It was driving me crazy.

"How long did you say we'd have to wait?" a kid with glasses and a tie wanted to know. He was standing with his hands clasped over his head, trying to keep the rain off.

"Eight minutes."

"Shoot! I should have stayed in the lecture hall and learned some more science."

The blond girl walked away. "Where are you going?" I called.

She half turned. "I can't stand waiting."

"It's raining, you'll get soaked."

"Who cares!" She flung her braid over her shoulder and moved briskly toward the corner.

"The bus is coming—wait!" I looked desperately up the street. Where was the bus? In a minute she'd be gone. *Do something,* I told myself. A gray van was rolling by slowly. I'd half noticed it parked up the street. I ran into the road and leaped up on the step of the van. The window was open on the passenger side. A man was driving. Next to him was a woman, her face hidden by a red kerchief and dark glasses. There were several full shopping bags on the seat between her and the man.

"Hi," I said, hanging onto the open window. "Give me a ride downtown?"

"No."

"Oh—you sure?"

"Yes."

"Get off!" the driver said. He was wearing dark glasses, too, and a knit cap pulled down over his forehead. A round, fleshy face. He didn't look at me, but I had a quick impression that I'd seen him someplace before.

Then, as I was ready to hop off, the woman changed her mind. "Okay, we'll give you a ride."

"What?" the man said. "Don't be—"

"Explain it to you later." She smiled at me. She had big white teeth. "You want a ride, hop in back, and make it fast."

I looked back at the blond girl. The van had carried me past her. "Terrific!" I said.

"The doors in back are unlocked."

"Thanks!"

I jumped off. The van pulled up ahead. I ran back to the girl. "Hey, I got us a ride." I pointed to the waiting van. "They're going to take us downtown." She hesitated.

I laughed. "I'm safe!"

"I'm not afraid!"

I opened the door, and she climbed into the van after me. At the same moment the three other kids who'd been waiting for the bus came running up.

"Give us a ride too?" the Black guy said.

"Sure," I said.

He and the boy with glasses got in. I took the dog from the little redheaded girl. She threw in her gym bag and climbed in. Then the woman came around the side, the red scarf pulled half over her face. She was taller than I'd thought, wearing a belted trench coat over dark jeans. "What's going on here?" she said.

"I said I'd give you a ride, Derek, not the whole freaking school."

"Oh, if that's the way it is," the blond girl said, "I'll walk." She started to get down.

"Me too," I said quickly, starting to follow her.

"No you don't," the woman said. She thrust the girl back into the van and slammed the door.

2

It was dark inside the van. I could hear the rain on the metal roof and the tires swishing over the wet pavement, a cozy sound. "Did you see the way she pushed me?" the blond girl said. She was sitting right next to me.

"She didn't hurt you, did she?" I said.

"That was gross, all right." It was the other girl, the small one with the poodle. "She's a crude person, you can tell. But they are giving us a ride. I'm glad to be out of that rain."

"How about her face when she saw all of us back here?"

"Looked like she was going to explode."

"Yeah!"

A little light filtered in through some bolt holes in one side of the van, and after a while I could just make out the others. Everyone was sitting on the floor except for the big guy, who was braced against the back. We were all talking over each other.

"Hey, it's dark in here, somebody turn on the light. Ha ha."

"She sure didn't want to take all of us. You hear what she said?"

"Must be worried about her precious truck."

"Materialistic!"

"Oooof, this floor is so uncomfortable—"

"Hard, you mean!"

I felt buoyant and excited. I was glad all these other kids had barged in. It was even better than if just the blond girl and I were alone. I'd think of a hundred terrific things to say and not get out one. But with the others around, it was like a party. I felt loose, really relaxed and easy.

"Hello, all you people out there in total darkness, I'm Derek Chapman."

"Hello, Derek! Which one are you?" That was the girl with the dog again.

"Uh—sorry to say, I'm the one who got you lucky folks this thrilling and unique ride."

"Well, that's okay, Derek, it's dry in here. Cocoa's glad, aren't you, Cocoa. I'm Wendy. Wendy Manheim. Who's this nice fellow sitting next to me?" She had a really bouncy way of speaking.

"Ed Hill here." He was the boy with the glasses, and the Black guy, standing up, was Jeff Wyatt. He was keeping to himself. Maybe he was one of those strong silent types, or maybe he was not feeling too friendly toward all these white faces.

"I'm Pam Barbushek," the blond girl next to me said.

"Barbushek—is that a Czech name?" I asked.

"Russian," she said briefly. "Does your dog bite, Wendy?"

"Cocoa's all bark and no bite. Besides, Pam Barbushek, he's right here in my lap, aren't you, baby? I wish I had a towel, he's so wet."

"Wring him out. Ha, ha." That was Ed, the one with glasses. Terrific sense of humor.

"You want a tissue?" Pam said.

"No, that's all right, I'll dry him with my scarf."

"Let me guess why you call your dog Cocoa," Ed said. "Because he's so sweet!"

"No, because he's so dark," Wendy said.

"You can't tell in here. We're all boogies in the dark. Ha, ha."

I couldn't believe it. What a jerk. I thought his type died off with Neanderthal Man. Jeff didn't say anything. You can never tell how people are going to react to things. But next to me Pam was muttering under her breath. I shifted a fraction closer and leaned my arm casually against the wall behind her. A fresh soapy smell came from her skin.

"Do you like bluegrass?" I said to her.

"Bluegrass?"

"Bluegrass music. Jug bands. Mountain music."

"I don't know anything about it."

"Bluegrass—they grow that in Kentucky, don't they?" Wendy said. "I have an aunt in Kentucky."

"Ole Ken-tuck," Ed said. "Thass where the ole darkies use to be."

Just then the van took a sharp turn and we were all thrown off balance. Someone landed heavily against me. Pam? I reached out. The dog was yipping, and the next thing I knew she was on my chest, slobbering around my face. "She's licking my ear!" I exclaimed. Everyone laughed.

"She can lick my ear next."

"Cocoa, come back here. Cocoa!"

I grabbed the dog. "I've got her, Wendy. Reach out." She was sitting across from me. Our hands touched.

"I wanna hold your hand," she sang. "I wanna hold your haa-aaaand!"

The dog was barking, and we were all laughing. There was a really friendly feeling. Then Ed yelled, "I can't find my glasses. They fell off." I could hear him patting the floor. "Where are they? Don't anybody move. I can't afford another pair."

"I can't see a thing in here," Pam said. "This is ridiculous. Hey, up front!" Her voice really carried. "Up front, there—turn on the light back here."

"No light," the woman called back. "Sorry."

I reached up along the wall. I could just make out a dome light overhead, but no bulb.

Ed was feeling around on his hands and knees. "Nobody move. Whatever you do, don't step on my glasses."

"I found them," Jeff said.

"Good boy," Ed said. "Thanks."

"Yeah, we boogies can see in the dark."

"Ha, ha," Ed said.

"Ha-ha yourself, you asshole."

There was dead silence. "About time," Pam muttered.

Ed peered through one of the tiny bolt holes in the wall. "I just saw the Hotel Rialto sign—"

"How can you tell?"

"He's got his glasses on."

"We're coming downtown. There's McDonald's—"

"You sure?" Jeff said.

"Sure I'm sure. McDonald's. The Big M."

"Okay, let me off," Jeff called. He knocked against the van wall. "Here's where I get off. Thanks for the ride!"

But the van didn't slow down.

"There's the library," Ed announced.

Pam stood up. "Hello, up there," she yelled. "Stop, please."

"In a minute," the woman called back. "Too much traffic. We'll circle around."

"I wanted to get out at the library," Pam complained. "I'm meeting my girlfriend."

I made a quick decision. "The library? That's where I'm getting off."

"They're circling around," Wendy said. "I guess I'll get out at the library, too, and catch a bus to the Field House."

We were all silent as the van made a right turn.

People started shifting around toward the back. We'd be going our separate ways soon.

The van suddenly lurched forward, throwing us all off balance. Pam fell back against me. I wasn't unhappy to have her in my arms.

"You all right?" I said.

"No!" She jerked free. "And if you want to be helpful, make your friends stop."

"I don't know what I can do," I said. "They're not my friends."

"Then how'd that nasty woman know your name?"

"What?" I had an uneasy desire to laugh, and then I felt suddenly scared. "Where'd you get that idea?"

"She called you by name," Pam said.

"No she didn't."

"You happen to be wrong. I distinctly heard her call you 'Derek.'"

"I'm sure she didn't!"

"Yes, she did—'Derek,'" Wendy said. "I heard her too."

"How could she? I don't know her. I never saw her before in my life."

"I don't care if you know her or not," Pam said. "I just want *out* of this vehicle."

"I don't get this," Ed said. He was peering through the bolt hole again. "What are we doing on the Expressway? We're going out of town. We're heading the wrong way."

I scrambled over legs and feet to the back and tried the rear doors. They were locked. The woman had locked us in. Why? When I'd jumped onto the step, she had said, "Get in, the doors are unlocked." I remembered that distinctly. And she *had* called me "Derek." Now I remembered that. How did she know me? My mind flashed to that *Time* article about Dad last year, with a picture of me, telling where I went to school. Dad had been teed off when he saw that. They hadn't asked his permission. There was a sour taste in my throat. Those people had been waiting for me!

But no, that was crazy. Paranoiac. *I* had asked *them* for a ride. The whole scene passed through my mind while I fruitlessly rattled the door handles. When I had jumped up and looked into the window, the driver had said, "Get off!" And then the woman suddenly changed her mind. And she'd said to the driver, "Explain it to you later."

The driver—there'd been something about him. I tried to remember his face, what little I'd seen of it. Just the profile. The cap pulled down low, the squashed nose . . . Then I knew. I started sweating. That flattened nose!

I'd seen that man before, seen him on the 12:22 bus a couple of Saturdays running. Usually the bus was empty when it picked me up, so I'd especially noticed him. He'd sat in back both times, alone, wearing dark glasses. I remembered thinking that he might be a boxer because of his nose. That interested me, and I wanted to get a look at his hands, but he seemed so forbidding that I never even tried to sit near him.

Kidnapped. The word, hardly a thought, rose in my

mind. Kidnapped. They'd been watching me. Waiting for the right moment. But all those other kids and the dog—it didn't make sense. I stood there, leaning my head against the cold metal doors, hearing the steady whine of the wheels, and I knew it was true. It was the thing I'd been dreading, fearing, even half waiting for, all my life.

3

"Hey up there! What are you doing?"

Everyone was yelling and shouting.

"Are you stupid?"

"Answer us, are you deaf?"

The high-pitched whine of the engine and the sound of tires swallowed up our shouts. I was yelling with the others, hoping against hope that there was some other explanation than the one I felt in my bones was right.

"Stop this van, please!"

"You're going to get into deep trouble—"

"Let me off, I'll get off here!"

Pam and Jeff were hammering on the sliding door separating the van from the cab.

"Shut up back there!" The man's rough voice rose over ours, silencing us.

"Who does he think he is?" Jeff muttered.

Wendy lit a cigarette. Yellow light flickered. "Anybody want a smoke?" she whispered.

"Don't smoke in here," Pam said. "You'll choke us all." Her voice was tense.

"I need a cigarette now," Wendy said. "I'm sorry! I'm supposed to be at the Field House right now to work out. I'm practicing for the All-State Gymnastic Meet. It's very important that I get enough practice. My coach is going to be furious."

"You're a gymnast?" Pam asked.

"Yes. Nadia Comaneci is my heroine. That Rumanian girl. I saw her in the 1976 Olympics in Montreal. She got a perfect ten."

"You went to Montreal!" Ed said. "I saw it on TV. You see that weight lifter? Man, he lifted five hundred pounds."

"I bet Comaneci doesn't smoke," Pam said. She pronounced the name "Co-man-ee-chi."

"Com-a-*netch*," Wendy said. "Com-a-*netch!* Don't you know anything?"

"Comaneechi or Coma*netch*," Pam said, "why don't you just put out that filthy cigarette!"

"Leave her alone," I said. "She's upset."

"We're all upset," Jeff said. "Who do these people think they are? It's my birthday, and I'm supposed to be meeting my girl right now."

"Your birthday," Wendy said. "How old are you?"

"Seventeen today."

"Happy birthday, anyway," she said. "What's your girl's name? What are you going to do to celebrate?"

"Well, if these maniacs ever cut out this game, I'm

taking Arletta to a matinee performance of Chekhov's *The Cherry Orchard* at the Repertory Theater."

He had a deep, resonant voice. He sounded like a radio announcer. "You an actor?" I said.

"The best, and getting better all the time!"

"I love plays," Wendy said. "Are you going to do anything afterward? Have a party?"

"We're meeting my parents at Aunt Marie's Cornucopia. They have the best Italian food anywhere."

"*You* like Italian food?" Ed said. "Hey, Goomba!"

"Yeah, 'Goomba,' I like Italian food. How about you?" Jeff's voice held a warning.

"Hey, Jeff," Wendy said quickly, "I thought you were eighteen at least."

"I've always been taken for older. How old are you, Wendy?"

"How old do I look?"

"About twelve," he said.

"Oh! Well, I'm fifteen, actually. And as far as I'm concerned, maturity has to do with the way you act, not how big or how tall you are. In the 'seventy-six Olympics Nadia weighed only eighty-six pounds, and she got a perfect ten!"

"No one is arguing with you, little lady," Jeff said.

"Oh, please! Don't give me that 'little lady' stuff. If I haven't had enough of that all my life! Peewee, half pint, the little giant—ugh! How old are you, Ed?"

"Fifteen. My birthday's in December." He had his eyes to a bolt hole again.

"December? So is mine," Wendy said. "December what?"

"Seventh. Pearl Harbor Day—when the Japs bombed Pearl Harbor, back in the Second World War. My father was in the Navy, stationed there."

"My birthday is December eighth," Wendy said. "Isn't that a coincidence! We were almost born on the same day. How old are you, Derek?"

"Sixteen. July fifteenth." This whole inane conversation was driving me crazy. Sooner or later I would have to tell them. I would have to say, *You've been kidnapped, and it's because of me.*

"How about you, Pam? How old are you?"

"I'm seventeen, and I don't see what that has to do with anything. Are you unreal or something? We're all being hijacked, and you're playing games!"

"Hey, we're really out in the country now," Ed said. "I can see fields. Man, these people are going to get in big trouble. My old man doesn't like anybody messing with his family."

"Tough," Jeff said, with that sarcastic edge to his voice. "Your family is really tough, fighting *Japs!* They ever burn any crosses?"

"Quit it, why don't you!" Pam said. "I'm trying to understand this. Why would anyone want to hijack *us?* There's nothing special about us. There has to be a rational explanation."

"Maybe it's a practical joke," Wendy said hopefully.

"What do you think, Derek?" Pam said. "You haven't said anything yet."

"It's no joke," I mumbled.

"I think you know more than you're letting on," Pam said.

"My old man's going to tear them up," Ed said. He began cracking his knuckles. "I was supposed to get home and help him work on the house. We're sheet-rocking the living room, and he can't do the work without me. It's a two-man job. That sheet rock kills, man. You need two men to handle that stuff. You'll bust your guts if you don't have two men—"

"Okay, okay! We heard it all!" Jeff said. "Other people have got people expecting them too."

"Let's not quarrel," Wendy said. "Right, Cocoa? Everybody, really, we shouldn't quarrel. I mean, they have to stop sometime, and then we'll get out—"

"Give me a puff of your cigarette," I said to her.

"Ugh!" Pam moved away from me. I took a couple of drags.

Kidnapping five of us didn't make sense. I knew why they wanted me—I was Jimmy Neal Chapman's son—but why the others? I went over everything that had happened. Everything I could put together.

"Listen, Derek." Pam gripped my arm. "Tell the truth now. You're in on this, aren't you?"

"No. What do you mean?" I pulled my knees up sharply.

"I have a hunch about this. I've read about psychological experiments done on people—putting them under pressure, seeing how they react, if they crack, that sort of thing. I've read about that in a psychology magazine. Is that what's going on?"

"That sounds sick," Wendy said.

"Sick? That's right! It's one of those stupid experiments," Pam said. "That's the way they think they can find out about people. Prove what a bunch of sheep people are. Like us! Jumping into this van, following the leader—I ought to have my head examined!"

"Look, you don't make any sense," Jeff said. "They didn't know we were going to be there at the bus stop. How could they? What if we didn't come to the lecture? My mom wanted me to stay home to watch my younger brother and sister. I almost did. Then she said schoolwork came first."

"Yeah, and I almost didn't come when I couldn't get my father's car started," Ed said. "I was planning to drive, so I wouldn't even have been waiting for the bus."

"Who you kidding?" Jeff said. "You can't drive at fifteen in New York State."

"Will you two stop that!" Pam said. "Who cares how we got there. Those people knew there was going to be a lecture. What's the big deal? There was an item in the paper about it the other night. A first for Payne School. Opens its doors to public-school students, blah, blah, blah. So they figured there'd be some kids waiting for the bus—that only makes sense." She continued stubbornly. "It's not us specifically they wanted, but any four or five kids. It was just a matter of getting us into the van. Derek got us in, remember?"

I got up and banged on the partition separating the cab from the back, hitting it so hard my hands stung. "Quit that!" the man yelled.

"Your buddy's talking," Pam said. I wondered why I'd ever thought I liked her. "You *were* following me, Derek, don't deny it! You got me in the van, and the rest of you followed. Probably, if you hadn't Derek would have called you. That's the way they figured it out, isn't it, Derek? Isn't it? Well, isn't it? There's nothing very mysterious here!"

"If I thought that was it, I'd—" Jeff said. "Who do you think you are, anyway? I'm nobody's guinea pig!"

Even though they had it all wrong, I felt guilty.

"That's crummy," Wendy said. "We're not guinea pigs! They've got no right to do this. It's like the Nazis and the Russians."

I leaned across the van and tangled my fingers in Cocoa's fur. "Take it easy," I said. "It isn't that way at all, Wendy." I felt like a real phony reassuring her. It was really worse than any of them thought.

"You're one of those Payne boys, aren't you?" Jeff said. "You're the only one in this van."

"I go to Payne School, yes."

"I knew the moment I saw you, with your English tweed jacket, your Swedish sneakers, and jeans. Humility combined with arrogant tastefulness."

"Oh, knock it off!" I said.

"Payne-in-the-ass School," Ed said. Then: "Did any of you ever stop to think that those two up front might be undercover cops?"

"Oh, come on!" Pam said.

"I mean it. They could be after drugs. These Payne School kids are into everything. They've got the money, and their parents don't tell them anything. They get everything they want. All the spending money. They don't know what it means to sweat for a dollar. So they pick us up. They think we're all Payne School, all a bunch of rich little snots like him."

"Why don't you all just shut up?" I said, suddenly enraged. "If I've got to be in this van with you, I don't want to listen to a lot of stupid talk. Somebody give me a piece of paper!" I snatched Pam's notebook and tore out a sheet. And in the dark, I scrawled, WE ARE KIDNAPPED.

"What are you doing?" Pam said. "Give me back my notebook!"

"Taking notes on the guinea pigs, Chapman?" Jeff said. "That part of the deal?"

GRAY VAN, I wrote. FIVE KIDS—PAYNE SCHOOL—TAKEN BY MAN AND WOMAN—HELP!

A match flickered. Wendy leaned over my shoulder. "We are kidnapped," she read aloud. "Kidnapped," she repeated.

"Kidnapped? That's crazy."

"Hey, what's going on here? What's he doing now?"

"Light another match, Wendy!"

I rolled up the paper into a thin tube and threaded

it through one of the bolt holes. The paper tore. In my frustration, I yanked it back, tearing it more, then rolled it up again.

"Hold a light for me, Wendy," I said, working the paper through the bolt hole. I didn't know what good it would do. Already I imagined the paper blowing away into a deserted field where no one would ever find it. It was like throwing a feather into the wind and hoping it would land in someone's hand.

"That was my last match," Wendy said. "We're in the dark again."

I slumped down on the floor. I could taste the fear in my mouth. "I might as well tell you. I should have told you before. We *have* been kidnapped. I'm not kidding. I mean, *I've* been kidnapped. All of you just had the bad luck to be with me."

"Kidnapped," Wendy said again. "I don't believe it. Why would anyone want to kidnap me? We don't have any money. All the money we have my parents saved for twenty years—"

"We don't have any money either," Ed said.

"It's not you. I told you it's not you. It's me. My father is Jimmy Neal Chapman."

"Well, my father is Charles Joseph Hill. Big deal!"

"You telling the truth?" Jeff said.

"Don't be an idiot. Would I joke about something like this?"

"Jimmy Neal Chapman," Pam said. "I read an article about Jimmy Neal Chapman for an economics report. They called him the Boy Millionaire, didn't they? His mother had a candy store in New York City."

"The Bronx," I said. "That was my grandmother, Fannie Neal Chapman."

Jeff whistled. "Ladies and gentlemen, we are in the hallowed presence of the son of an American legend. From rags to riches. Poor boy makes good. Horatio Chapman. Mr. Money himself."

"I still don't know who his father is," Ed said.

Jeff laughed. "You mean how much is he worth? Plenty, boy, plenty. You ever hear of the Big C hamburger chain? They're big all through the South and West? That's Chapman money. And the Chapman packing houses? And Chapman frozen foods?"

Wendy leaned across toward me and tapped me on the arm. "Derek. Are you really rich?"

I nodded. "My father is."

"How rich?" Ed said. "You don't look that rich to me."

"It still doesn't make sense," Pam said. "If they wanted you, why'd they take all of us? That's stupid."

"They didn't know they were going to get you all. They must have been watching me—I don't know for how long, maybe for months. The man—I've seen him on the bus Saturdays. I take that same bus every Saturday downtown. They only had to get to Payne Road before the bus and grab me. Nobody's ever at that stop but me. I'm sure that was their plan. Then they saw you all—they didn't expect you. They must have agreed to wait for another Saturday, and they were rolling past me, maybe slow enough for the woman to get a good look at me too, when I jumped on the step and practically begged them to grab me."

"Boy, how stupid!" Ed said. "You kidnapped yourself."

"If what you're saying is true," Pam said, "they had to take you once you got on that step. Because *you* saw *them*. If they went away and came back, the next time you'd recognize them. You'd be wary. On guard. And that wouldn't do."

Ed cracked his knuckles. "My father was laid off at G.E. last fall. We're on unemployment. He's still waiting to be called back."

"Derek," Wendy said, "you're making it all up, aren't you?"

I felt so tired, almost too tired to think. "I wish I was," I said. "I wish it was all make-believe, but it's not!"

They all moved away from me then as if they carried Geiger counters and I was radioactive.

"When I was a little kid," I continued, "I used to be scared all the time that I was going to be kidnapped. Every night when I went to sleep, I thought the kidnappers were going to come while I was sleeping—"

"Every kid thinks that," Jeff put in. "You don't have to be rich. It's a common fantasy. Burglars, robbers, kidnappers—"

"No," I said, "I was never afraid of robbers, just kidnappers. I thought they'd come and take me away in a sack." I wanted them to know that being kidnapped was something that really happened to rich kids. When I was ten years old I collected newspaper stories about kidnappings. I had a cigar box full of them. A banker's daughter had been drugged and found in a gutter. Another girl, whose father was a corporation president, had been buried alive in a coffin for ten days before they found her. Two brothers, whose father was vice-president of an airline, had been tied to trees and left in the woods. The younger one died of exposure.

One gruesome story after another. *You're next, Derek Chapman,* I used to think. "I still read those kidnap stories," I said. "There was that oil man's grandson. They sliced off his ear and sent it home to his mother."

"Ugh," Ed said. "Don't talk that way in front of girls."

"I was terrified I'd be kidnapped before my eleventh birthday," I said. "It came on Friday the thirteenth that year. But when my birthday passed and I was still safe, my mood swung around. I told myself that so many other people were being kidnapped, they'd never find me."

"You wanted to think that," Jeff said. "You wanted to think you were invisible. Money is never invisible!"

Ed started swearing. It was finally sinking in. That's right, Ed Hill, I've been kidnapped and you've been kidnapped too!

The van slowed down, made a sharp turn. We bumped and jounced over a dirt road. Rocks hit the bottom of the van, and dust seeped in. On and on we went.

Finally the van halted. The cab doors slammed. We heard voices outside. Cocoa started whining. "She's scared," Wendy said. Ed had his eye to the peephole again. "They're going away!"

"Listen, everybody," Pam said. "Let's stick together. When they come, nobody get out. Just refuse to get out. They can't do anything to us if we stick together."

I wondered if Pam was afraid. For a moment, I wanted very much to touch someone. Faintly we heard the sound of glass breaking. After a while there were steps outside again.

The back of the van was opened. Light flooded in. I squinted. It was the woman in the red scarf. She wore a green surgical mask over her mouth. "Okay, kids, you're coming out one at a time." Her voice was muffled. "Don't anybody move till I say so." She was holding a gun. "Derek!"

Slowly I stood up and moved forward. The gun made everything real. I saw trees, a frozen lake, a bark-covered lodge. Then a black plastic bag was thrust over my head. The plastic pressed against my face; it clung to my nose and mouth when I breathed. I was suffocating. I tried to rip it off.

"Keep your hands down!" The man grabbed me and led me away from the van. I stumbled. I heard the gun click. And what I thought was, They're going to kill me.

4

Prodded forward. Stumbling. Prodded forward again. My arm twisted behind my back. I was going to be shot, but my mind was clear. This is it, Derek, they're going to kill you. You're going to die. I said it to myself as clearly as that. Then I thought that on both sides of my family people lived to be very old. My great-grandmother Chapman died when she was ninety-seven. I'd be the first one to die at sixteen.

Pushed again.

"Up!" the man's muffled voice ordered.

I didn't understand. Up what? I banged into something, stumbled, then understood. Steps. One . . . two . . . three . . . I fell forward. Caught myself. Pushed again. Inside a building. The dank smell of stale air. *Click.* The gun! I was trembling.

"Get him upstairs," the woman said. I thought, He won't kill me in front of a woman. It seemed to make sense.

I was pushed up a flight of stairs. Into another room. Pushed into a chair, my hands pulled behind me. They looped rope around my body. I could feel their heat, smell them. They were sweating. They didn't say anything.

Suddenly I heard a terrific racket from outside, yelling and hammering. I thought, They've come! We're going to be rescued. We're going to be free! Then I heard Cocoa barking, and realized it was the other kids in the van. They were shouting, pounding on the sides of the van.

The man cursed. "Pearl, dammit—!" The floor creaked under his weight.

"Bogie, what are you going to do?"

"Shut those stupid kids up!"

I heard him go down the stairs, the woman after him. Pearl and Bogie, I thought dazedly. Frankie and Johnny. Bonnie and Clyde. Too much. It was chokingly hot inside the plastic bag. I shook the ropes loose, got my hands free, and tore the plastic bag off my head.

I ran down the stairs. The windows were boarded up. It was a big room, dim, too dark to see much. I sensed more than saw couches, a long wooden table, the bulk of a fieldstone fireplace filling one wall. I started for the door, but before I reached it I heard footsteps on the porch. I flung myself down behind the couch, tasting dust in my throat. Feet approached the couch. His feet. I pressed my face into the dust.

"Please, I'm suffocating." It was Wendy. "Please, take this bag off my head, I can't breathe. I have asthma."

"Shut up," the man said. *Slap!* Wendy cried out. Their footsteps went up the stairs. I crept around the side of the couch. The door was open. I saw trees. I started running, still crouched over. I sprinted for the porch, slipped on the wet steps outside, and went sprawling.

There was a yell from above. "Pearl! He's gone!"

I heard him pounding down the stairs.

I scrambled to my feet and ran for the trees.

He was behind me. *Don't look back. Get into the woods.* He was yelling. I thought he was going to shoot. I zigzagged, plunged into the trees. I looked back. I'd lost him. *Hide!* I threw myself down behind the upturned roots of a fallen tree, catching my breath. Overhead I heard the wind in the bare trees. Then rustling sounds. Chipmunks? Was that what chipmunks sounded like? Or was it him? I could feel my heart beating against the ground. Slowly I raised my head. Where was he? Was he waiting too? Waiting for me to make the first move?

I couldn't stay here. Too close to the road. If he circled around, he could come up behind me. Or maybe he was on the road, waiting for me to step out of the woods. I started creeping deeper into the trees, trying not to make a sound. I was going to get away. They weren't going to grab me again. I'd go so deep in the woods they'd never find me. Then I'd get help. Without me, they'd have to let the other kids go.

Behind me I heard a noise. I froze. The wind? An animal? Then a twig snapped, so close that my heart jumped. I twisted around. He was right behind me. He flung himself toward me and grabbed my jacket. I ripped free. Ran. Veered toward the road. I could run on the road, outrun him. The trees thinned. I saw the van, the road . . . another step and I'd be past the van. *Free.*

The woman burst out from behind the van. She threw her arms around me and kicked me to the ground. She was all over me, pressing me into the ground. Then he was on me, screaming and pounding me. He punched me in the face. Nobody had ever hit me like that in my life. My face went numb.

She made him stop hitting me and told him to get me upstairs. He dragged me into the house and up the stairs, then threw me into a chair and slapped me around some more before he tied me up.

Wendy stared at me. She sucked in her lips. Her sweater was bunched up under the ropes. Her green scarf was dangling. She looked dazed. Cocoa whimpered in her lap.

They brought up the others one by one and tied them to chairs, hands lashed behind their backs, ankles taped to the chair legs.

"What happened to your face?" Pam was tied up next to me. "You're covered with blood," she whispered. "What did they do to you?"

"They beat me." My throat filled.

"Beasts!" she whispered fiercely. "Take these ropes off me!" she cried, twisting against the ropes.

"You want to be gagged?" the woman said. She had a flat, emotionless voice.

As they tied each of us up they took all our possessions, our wallets, watches, and rings. They threw down books and notebooks, and emptied Wendy's gym bag. The man found Jeff's theater tickets, examined them, then tossed them on the pile. He pocketed the money in Jeff's wallet. "You do all right on welfare." He forced a ring with a large red stone from Jeff's finger.

"That ring's not worth anything to you," Jeff said. "It was my brother's, his birthstone. He's dead now."

"Boo-hoo," the man said, tossing the ring to Pearl. He yanked a thin silver chain with a six-pointed star from around Wendy's neck. He held it up in the air. "What's this?"

"A star of David," Wendy said.

"You a Jew girl?"

"I'm Jewish, yes." She bit her lip. "My mother's got a heart condition, you've got to let me go. She's not well, she can't get upset." The woman pulled the gold earrings from Pam's ears.

Were they taking every bit of identification from us before they killed us? He picked up my wallet and went through the contents, examining everything. Besides all the junk I carried, there were photos of Mom and Ora, and one of Dad standing beside his sports Mercedes. I hated to have him look at my family, but what really upset me was when he held up the three foil-wrapped prophylactics I'd been carrying around ever since my sixteenth birthday. I don't know why I carried them, except that it made me feel I was ready for anything.

Maybe I'd seen too many movies. I didn't really think things happened the way you saw in movies— not about sex, not about anything. If they did, by now I would have wiped out the man and woman and freed us all. Instead I was as helpless as a baby; I couldn't even stop them from pawing through my personal things.

"Hey, Pearl, look at this," he said. "Rubbers! The dirty kid!"

I tried to catch Pam's eyes. I didn't want her to get the wrong idea.

"What do you bet he doesn't even know what to do with them," Bogie said. Pearl snickered. "Look at him, he's turning red just like a girl. What do you do, Derek, fill them with water and drop them out the window?"

He emptied my wallet and counted the money. Just a few days before, I'd received my monthly allowance.

"You always walk around with a hundred bucks in your pocket?" He circled my chair, waving the money in my face. "The rest of these kids didn't have twenty-five bucks between them. It must be nice to be filthy rich. What is this, your Coke money?"

I licked my lips. They were puffed up. My face was really beginning to hurt.

"A hundred bucks," Ed said, looking over at me.

"My old man doesn't collect that much unemployment insurance."

"You're not a rich pig," the woman said. She was strapping my watch to her wrist. "I always wanted a watch with a calendar. Bet it glows in the dark, too." She held out her arm to the man.

"Nice," he said. "There's a lot more where that came from."

"My mother gave that to me for my birthday," I said. Right away I was sorry I said anything. My whole face filled with emotion. On the back Mom had had the watch inscribed: *For my one, only, and forever son, Derek.*

"Stop blubbering. Your daddy will buy you another one and give you some more play money," the man said. "If he has anything left after he takes care of us."

"Can I have my wallet back now?"

"Keep your mouth shut." The woman dropped the wallet on the floor with the other stuff. "We're going downstairs now. I don't want a peep out of any of you." She went down the line, looking at each of us in turn. "You understand?" Those colorless eyes. That flat voice. She grabbed Wendy by the hair and yanked her head back and forth. "No noise. Nothing." A whimper broke from Wendy's lips. The woman pulled her head back farther. "Ughhh . . . *please*," Wendy cried. Cocoa crept into a corner, whining nervously.

"*No noise,* or I gag you all!" One last look, and they both left.

Wendy moaned softly.

"I don't believe it," Pam whispered.

Ed had a frozen expression on his face, and Jeff stared off at a wall. It was like the aftermath of an accident. We were all stunned.

5

My mouth was dry . . . so dry.

I was thirsty. I licked my lips and tasted blood. The ropes cut into my wrists. Blood was caked in my nose. It was unreal. Only hours ago I'd been bugging Greenie and planning what to do with my afternoon. Greenie— I felt a wash of warmth. I wished I'd been a little nicer today.

I tried to move my chair. The whole attic was full of chairs. There were boxes shoved under the eaves, mattresses, bureaus, and more chairs stacked on top of one another. A little light came from diamond-shaped windows set close to the peak at each end of the attic. The only other openings were wooden louvers beneath the windows, at floor height. I was tied up next to one of these louvers.

I tipped my chair backward a little and looked down through the tilted slats. I saw a path, a tree trunk, rocks, the edge of a gravel driveway. I wondered whose summer place this was that they'd broken into.

Next to me, Pam twisted back and forth, muttering to herself.

There were steps on the stairs. "They're coming," Pam said. Cocoa, who'd been lying at Wendy's feet, stood up, arched almost like a cat, and growled in her throat.

"Cocoa," Wendy said. "Cocoa, no! Cocoa, be quiet. Come here, baby, come here—"

The woman walked around behind us, checking the ropes. She still wore the green surgical cone over her mouth. If I saw her in a crowd, would I recognize her? Yes, I thought, those cold, pale, impersonal eyes—I'd know them again.

"Can't you loosen these ropes?" Pam asked.

Cocoa yipped at the woman from under Wendy's chair.

"Can I have a drink?" I said. "I'm dying of thirst."

"What's your home phone number?" she said.

"It's unlisted."

"Don't act stupid, I know that." From behind the green cone, her voice was edgy. "Your phone number!"

"Circle five—six nine eight seven." I hated telling her.

She wrote it down in a small brown spiral notebook, then called down the stairs, "Bring me up a drink, will you?"

The man came up with a can of beer. She turned, dropped the mask, and drank. I watched her. "Can I have some water?" I said. She dropped the can on the floor. The last drops trickled out.

"What's the make of your sneakers, your shirt, your jeans?" she asked.

"What?" I stared at her face. She hadn't pulled up the mask again.

"Check it, Bogie," she ordered.

The man twisted the collar of my shirt. "John Dant," he said. She wrote it down.

"I'm wearing Levi's," I said before he could unzip my jeans. "But if you want this for my father, he doesn't know anything about my clothes."

"Maybe not, and maybe he does," she said. "When we call and tell him we have you and we want the cash, I don't want any doubts in his mind that we have the merchandise."

It was the first time they'd actually said they were holding me for ransom.

"Where did you find out about me?"

"We know all about you and your father," she said. "Chapman Enterprises: a plastics company, a motor-manufacturing plant, a packing house. You live in a penthouse with white rugs in every room. Original paintings, and David Smith sculptures on the terrace."

She said it as though she'd been there, but I recognized the things that had been written in the *Time* article on Dad with color photos of our apartment. Dad should never have let those magazine people into our home. Mom wouldn't have. She was almost paranoid about privacy. She never wanted anyone to know where we were or what we were doing.

"Dad will believe you," I said.

"You bet he will. He'll believe me, because we've got the goods."

Goods. Merchandise. That was me. As if I were a thing, not a person.

"Look," Ed said, "my name is Ed Hill. I haven't got anything to do with this guy. I don't even know him. I never saw him before today. You could just let me go, I wouldn't tell anyone anything."

"Don't be disgusting," Pam said. "They're not going to let you go."

"But if you could just call our parents, tell them we're all right—" Ed persisted.

The woman swung around on him. "This is our business! Keep your mouth shut, or I'll shut it for you." She stared at him for a moment, then turned back to me. "Now, Derek, I want you to tell me something that nobody else knows about you. Nobody but you and your father. Not something a million people have read in the papers." She snapped her fingers. "Well? Come on, come on! Do you have a special nickname in the family?"

I shook my head.

"No nickname? No pet name?"

"No."

"What about your sister?" the woman said. "What about Ora?"

My heart jumped. Had they thought of kidnapping Ora? I glanced over at Wendy. She was sitting between Pam and Ed. She reminded me a little of Ora— they were about the same size.

Ora and I had been close when we were little, but after the separation things changed. We didn't see that much of each other. Just this past year, we started writing. Her letters were always breezy and always left me laughing. I'd gotten the last one only a few weeks ago, and had read it so many times I had memorized it.

> *Dear Elder Bro,*
>
> *And how are you? I am frankly rotten. Rotting away at the heart from too much Cal sun & juicy healthy wholesome friends. Ma mère says I am a corrupt Eastern child, influence of smog on formative years no doubt, and should learn to appreciate wholesome Cal girls. Morals not so wholesome, however. Sound interesting? Come see. Yum Yum. Yr. sis,*
>
> *Ora Bora.*

"How about a family name for your sister?"

I almost said it. Ora Bora. A wordplay on "aurora borealis." Because when she was a little girl, Ora had been so vivid, bright and shining, flashing across all our lives like the northern lights. She was the light one; I was always the darker one, quieter, soberer, less optimistic, moodier. Ora had taken our parents' divorce really hard, whereas I had somehow felt that I always knew it was coming.

"No pet name," I said. Ora Bora came from a time when our family was all together. It was none of their business. "My family doesn't have pet names. Or pets, either."

The others were watching and listening. I felt them judging me. Felt their scorn and hostility. They blamed me for all of this. If it wasn't for me, they wouldn't be here.

"All right, Derek, now let's quit fooling around. You know what I'm after. Give me a detail, something just you and your father know."

"Do you want to know what he eats for breakfast?" I asked.

"Try me."

"First about three cups of coffee, and then a bowl of oatmeal."

"Stuff it!" the man said. "What're you talking about? They probably printed that oatmeal crap in twenty-five articles about your father already. Oatmeal. Next you'll tell us he shines his own shoes and walks to work."

Cocoa was nervous. She circled the room, whining and sniffing. Once she came too close, and the woman kicked her away.

The woman leaned over me. "Come on, Derek, think," she said softly. "What about your room at home? You have something there that only you and your father know about?" Her fingers dug into my shoulders. There was a little froth of saliva at the corners of her mouth.

My mind slipped back to my room at home, with the windows opening onto our terrace, filled with potted trees and bushes, and the Smith sculpture that looked like a shield. I had books in my room, a radio, TV, the phone by my bed, the usual junk. There was a model airplane hanging from the ceiling. It had a remote-control engine. Years ago I'd flown it in Central Park. Now it just hung in the room, spinning slowly in the currents of air.

"Derek! Come *on!*" She slapped my face. I felt the blood rush to my cheek. "Think!"

"How can I think when you're hanging all over me? My circulation is cut off, my hands are numb. I can't think this way!"

My outburst set off the others.

"These ropes are too tight!"

"I'm thirsty!"

"When can we go to the bathroom?" Jeff asked.

"I want quiet here!" Pearl grabbed Jeff by the ear and shook him, as if she meant to shake his head off. "I don't care about your aches and pains, your sniffles and itches. We're not here to hold your hands. You are all, with the exception of Derek, here by chance. Unlucky for you. We didn't ask you to get into the van, but once you did, you were stuck. There's no way in the world that you can get away till we have what we're here for. You understand?"

She paused as if she expected questions, but no one responded. She released Jeff and continued. "Derek is our prize, our little gold nugget. Our solid gold kid. The rest of you aren't worth two cents. So the less you say, the less you get in our way or ask us stupid questions, the better off you are!" Her face had turned red, sweaty, and coarse.

Cocoa yipped shrilly at her.

She turned to the man. "Do something with that stupid dog!"

The man lunged. Cocoa ran in circles, barking even louder.

"Don't chase her," Wendy said. "She's not used to you. Here, Cocoa, honey, come to me, come to Wendy." She whistled softly, and Cocoa came to her chair.

"Are you thinking, Derek?" the woman said.

I nodded, still watching the man.

He grabbed Cocoa by the scruff, twisted his hand cruelly through her collar, and carried her out of the room.

"Where are you going?" Wendy cried. "Please! Please, I'll keep her quiet. Bogie, Mr. Bogie, please—"

We could hear Cocoa's strangled cries.

She was so little, like a toy. She reminded me of the stuffed animals I slept with when I was small. BooBoo the Soft was my favorite—a stuffed yellow dog.

I still had BooBoo, lying on my bed at home, one ear chewed off, his velvet nose dangling by a thread. Every time Dad noticed him, he'd say, "Old BooBoo the Soft still in residence, Derek?" And every time I'd promise to throw him in the incinerator. But I never did. My room wouldn't be the same without BooBoo the Soft flopping on the bed.

"Where's he taking Cocoa?" Wendy said frantically. "If you'd just let her stay with me, put her in my lap, I'd keep her quiet. I promise! She's not used to strangers, that's why she barks." Her voice quivered. "Please don't take her away, she'll be so scared. She's really a good little d—"

The woman snatched the green scarf from Wendy's neck and stuffed it into her mouth. "I told you to shut up," she said, as calmly as if she were talking about the weather.

Wendy's eyes bulged. She gave a strangled cough and spat out the gag. "Don't!" she cried. "I can't breathe that way."

The woman forced her head back and gagged her again, knotting the scarf tightly behind her head.

I had to turn away. "I thought of something," I said. Wendy was moaning and thrashing around. "I thought of what you could tell my father when you call, something no one else knows." I told her the name of Boo-Boo the Soft. "Now will you take that gag out of her mouth?"

"BooBoo the Soft," the woman said. "What's that supposed to mean?"

"It was a stuffed animal I had. BooBoo the Soft."

"Why in anyone's name would your father remember that?"

"Because I still have it on my bed at home."

"Oh, that's wonderful! That's really too thweet for words."

I looked away, down through the louver. Bogie was on the path, swinging Cocoa back and forth by the collar. The dog's legs pawed desperately at the air.

"All you other kids hear that about thweet little Derek's thweet little teddy bear?" the woman said. "BooBoo the Soft."

The man dashed Cocoa against the tree trunk. Once . . . twice . . . three times . . . Vomit rose in my throat.

"Well, Derek," the woman said, "I'm going out now to call Daddy-waddy and tell him about BooBoo the Soft." She was still snickering as she went down the stairs.

"Derek," Pam said. "Derek, open your eyes. What's the matter with you?"

I shook my head, afraid to speak. Afraid I'd cry it out to Wendy.

"Don't let her stupid teasing get to you. You look absolutely sick. Don't be so sensitive! They're stupid. They're both stupid and vicious."

I swallowed hard. What kind of people were they? If they could kill a harmless little dog in cold blood, they were capable of anything.

Sweat beaded Wendy's face. Her eyes rolled frantically. She wrenched against the ropes. "Don't fight it," Ed said. "You only make it worse. Look, look what you're doing to yourself. You're just getting yourself all upset."

Once, years ago, Ora had had a terrible asthma attack. I could still hear her shallow, wheezing, desperate gasps. My mother had carried her into the bathroom and turned on the hot faucet in the shower full force to ease the choking congestion in Ora's lungs. Who would care if Wendy couldn't breathe? Who would come? Not either of those people. My heart galloped sickeningly. They had murdered Cocoa. They were entirely capable of letting Wendy choke to death in that chair.

6

I strained at the ropes, twisting my arms back and forth. I tried to thread my wrists through the knots. I was going to free myself, take that gag out of Wendy's mouth, and free everyone. Then I'd break out through the louver and drop to the ground outside. I had to get away. I was the one the kidnappers needed. Once I was gone, they would have to let the others go.

"What are you doing! Who's making that noise?" Ed said. "You'll get us all in a jam making that racket. Cut it out!"

"I can't just sit here," I said, struggling futilely against the ropes.

"It's easy for you," Ed said. His glasses glittered in the fading light. "It's always easy if you've got the money. But what have the rest of us got? Beans. B-E-A-N-S! You can do what you want, they'll treat you with kid gloves. The rest of us have to do things their way, cooperate—"

"That's so stupid," Pam said. "Wait till they beat

you up! Let's get them up here. Make them do something!"

Wendy moaned. She was rocking back and forth. She'd been making these awful noises ever since they'd gagged her.

"If we all scream together—" Pam began.

"Forget it!" Jeff said. "There's nothing we can do. What are you grandstanding for?" Every time he opened his mouth his words sounded like lines from a play. "We are their prisoners. Our hands are tied. Talk is cheap, but this is real, in case you haven't noticed."

"Oh, I've noticed." Pam's cheeks were flaming. "I've noticed, all right. I've noticed how concerned people are about other people. Look at poor Wendy!"

"What do you want us to do?" Jeff said. "We're all helpless. I don't see you performing any miracles, Wonder Woman."

"I had you figured differently," she said. "I thought you had backbone—"

"Yes, that's me. Othello. The Noble Black who'll kill himself with a smile for frail white womanhood."

"Oh, shut up!" Pam said furiously.

"Make up your mind to it, they're not releasing us till they get their money," Jeff said.

"When's that going to be, rich boy?" Ed said. "How long's that going to be, rich boy? Huh, rich boy?"

"Don't call me that."

"What's the matter, don't you like the truth?"

"My name is Derek."

"What's wrong with calling you 'rich boy'? That's what you are. You ashamed that you're loaded, rich boy?"

"I said, my name is Derek!"

The bickering and hostility really made me frantic to be free. We were like five animals penned together, spitting and snarling.

It was fate, I told myself, and I thought of fate like a giant hand scooping up the five of us, squeezing us together in this unbearable, hateful intimacy. Five people who would never have known each other otherwise, or wanted to know each other. Now each of us wanted only to be safe, to be out of this horror, *free*—and the hell with everybody else!

We were all rationalizing like mad. Me, too. I had told myself that *I* ought to escape, because the others were in no danger, while Ed had figured things out exactly the opposite. The truth was, nobody gave a damn for anybody else.

"Everyone, be quiet!" Pam said. "Listen."

They were fighting downstairs. We could hear them clearly.

"What do you mean, feed them," Bogie was complaining. "What am I, a freakin' restaurant?"

"Take it easy," she said. "No big deal—just give them each some bread and a hunk of bologna."

"We don't have enough food to feed that whole gang." We heard him stomping around. "How long is this deal going to take? We didn't get enough food to feed all of those slobs up there."

"I'll buy more when I go out—"

"No you won't! You know what we said. We're not doing anything to make anyone remember us. The less places you're seen, the better off we are. We said that, didn't we?"

"Yes, but—"

"Yes, but—yes, but," he mimicked ferociously. "But what? We didn't invite that bunch along. Let them go hungry for a few hours. I've gone hungry plenty of times. Christ, I don't like this! We planned everything. It was supposed to go off just according to plan. We take one kid. We tie up one kid. We buy food for us and one kid. We figured it all out. Now look what we've got!"

"You're right, honey, but what choice did we have? Once those other kids got in—"

"The hell with them! They've messed us up good. Why should I feed them? I don't give a frig about them!"

"Okay, okay, don't get excited. Feed them or don't feed them, who cares! Just stay cool. You going to be okay? I should go out. You all right?"

"What do you think's wrong with me? You think I can't breathe without you holding my hand?"

"Don't start on me, Bogie."

"Well, just back off, give me room. Don't crowd me!"

"You want to forget the whole thing? Just forget it?"

"You must be nuts!" he exclaimed. "What are you talking about now?"

"I don't care," she said. "Let them go. Send them all home or leave them here, I don't care! Let's go. Come on, we'll go right now. We'll forget the whole thing. You go back to that wrecking yard, you can work there the rest of your life. I'm doing all this for you. What do I care? I don't need this grief, I'd just as soon forget the whole thing."

"Christ, and you're supposed to be the smart one! Let them go and the cops will be on us in a minute. That's it. That'll be it. The rest of my life in jail, you mean. That what you want, Pearl? Are you stupid or something?" he shouted.

He sounded as if he were in a real rage. Pam and I looked at each other. Then a door slammed downstairs. I looked out the louver. It was dark already. I could just make out the woman as she passed. She was going to call my father. Maybe we'd be out of this hell by morning.

Moments later the engine of the van turned over, and almost simultaneously there was a loud strangled sound from Wendy, more awful than anything before, as if she were dying.

"Somebody do something!" I was too far away. Wendy was between Ed and Pam. "Can't you bite the gag off?"

Ed scraped his chair next to Wendy's. Pam was trying to quiet her. Wendy's head was jumping back and forth like a puppet's. "Stop jerking around," Pam said. "Come on, we're trying to help you."

"Can he do it? Is he loosening the gag?" I couldn't see what Ed was doing. "Get your teeth on it. Bite it!"

"Shut up," Pam said. "He's trying."

Wendy was holding herself still now, but whimpering.

"Someone's coming," Jeff warned. "One of the ghouls."

Bogie burst into the attic and shone a blinding light in my face, then swung it around to the others. "What's all the freakin' noise?" The light made his head appear huge and swollen, like an evil tortoise. It was the first time that day that I'd seen him without the nose mask. A fleshy face, a lot of cheek, that flattened nose—a fat face. A fat, jowly, stupid face. Poppa Ghoul.

The light lingered on Wendy. Ed had gotten back in time. Wendy was quiet.

"Why don't you take that thing out of her mouth?" Pam said. "She's all right—she's not going to make any more noise."

Bogie's light blinded me. "What do you say, Chapman?"

"Pam's right. Can we have something to drink?" I was so dry I wanted to drink and drink, drink a gallon of water, a barrel of water. "Will you get me a drink?"

"Sure. Anything else, Your Majesty? You know what I got to do to get water? Take a bucket down to the lake, fill it, and then tote it back up here. You think

I'm going to do that for you? You want me to do that for you?"

"We're all thirsty," Jeff said.

Bogie swung the light to Jeff. "What did you say?" He had the gun in his belt.

"I've just got to have something to drink. How about it?"

Bogie emptied a beer. "You want a beer?" He licked his lips and tossed the can into a corner. "Pain-in-the-ass kids."

"I need a bathroom," Pam said. "You can't leave us tied up like this. We're not a bunch of animals."

"I can do anything I want. Did I ask you dopes to come barging in on us?"

"People have certain needs," Pam said. "You want us to do it on the floor?"

The man half smiled. "Sure, tiger cat, you do it anywhere you want to."

"That's disgusting," Pam said, her voice trembling. "You're disgusting!"

"Shut up!"

"You got to let us use the bathroom, man," Ed said in a placating voice. "We're not going to give you any trouble."

"No kidding?" Bogie said. "Is that right? Suppose all you kids shut up and let me run things around here. There's only one of you knows how to keep her mouth shut." He loosened Wendy's gag and flashed his light full in her face. "You going to give me any more trouble?"

She shook her head. She worked her mouth from side to side, grimacing and gulping air. She didn't say a word.

"I'm going to take you kids to the john, one at a time. One of you gives me any trouble and I'll let you all float away in your own juice."

He untied Wendy. "Where's Cocoa?" she whispered.

"The dog's in the boathouse. She's better off than you."

"Did you give her some water?"

"Sure thing. And a big bowl of Alpo. Come on!"

We could hear them moving around downstairs.

"Don't close the door." Bogie's voice drifted up to us clearly. "And don't flush." Wendy must have said something in that little whisper. "I don't care! Do it with the door open or do it in your pants. All the same to me."

When they came back, he retied Wendy. She didn't say a word, but after he'd taken Ed downstairs she whispered, "I've never been tied up in my life. I can't bear it. I have to be free. I've always used my body. I'm a gymnast. I don't even sleep quietly in one position. My mother says I'm moving all night." Her voice was beginning to quaver.

"None of us like it," Pam said.

"And I'm so worried about Cocoa. I haven't heard her barking. I don't trust that ugly man."

"Cocoa's all right," Pam said. "They've just got her tied up someplace—the boathouse, he said. Dogs are used to being tied up."

"She's more like a person than a dog. She's a member of our family, practically. I've had her nearly all my life."

When Ed came back, the man took Jeff down. Ed said, "The guy isn't all that bad. He seems regular, you can talk to him. It just proved what I said before, they're not going to hurt us if we keep our noses clean. They're after one thing, money. And who can blame them? If we had the nerve, we'd all do the same thing."

"Speak for yourself." Pam's rope of hair snapped over her shoulder. "I don't understand you. Those two have no standards. They're immoral," she said passionately. "They think they can have anything they want. They don't care who they trample on."

"Don't tell me you wouldn't grab a million bucks if you had a chance. Ahh, don't shake your head. Yes you would. You're no better than the rest of us."

"Don't even talk to me! You're blind to anything but your own narrow, stupid, selfish, *ignorant* point of view."

"Shhh," Wendy said anxiously.

"Ahh, get off your soapbox," Ed threw back. "You've got a big mouth. I feel sorry for your family. I bet you can't get any guy to come within a city block of you. You must scare them all off."

Pam's chin shot up. She compressed her lips. If looks could kill, Ed would have been dead.

I was the last one to be taken to the bathroom. Bogie rushed me down the stairs. His light flashed through the rooms. I saw a stuffed white ermine on the wall, and next to it an empty gun rack. In the bathroom, the toilet had not been flushed. I finished as fast as I could.

"I saved the latrine detail for you. Our million-dollar kid." He stood at the door the whole time, the gun in his belt. "Flush," he ordered. There was a pail of water on the floor. I scooped water into my mouth. He aimed a kick at my rear. "Who gave you permission? Flush!" I emptied the pail into the bowl.

Upstairs, he retied me. Being tied up again was awful. I felt depressed. I wished I could fall asleep and not wake up till this was all over.

"How about a little food?" Jeff said. "I'm pretty hungry—"

"I'm not your servant, darky." Bogie put his fist against Jeff's mouth, pushing his head back. "Keep your big black mouth shut. Got it?"

"You could loosen our ropes," Ed said. "We're not going to do anything. We can't get away."

"I'll think about it," Bogie said. He pointed his light at Wendy. "What's your father do, curly locks? I want to see if I can trust you."

"He works for the city."

"Go on."

"In the water department. He used to be a meter reader, a long time ago. Now he drives a truck."

"Wait a minute, hold on. I thought you told me you were a Jew."

"I beg your pardon?"

"Listen to the Jew girl. 'I beg your pardon,'" he mimicked. "Since when do Jews drive trucks? Your father owns the truck. He don't drive a truck."

Wendy's voice wavered. "I don't know what you mean. My father does so drive a truck. It's not his. He's worked for the city all his life. He and my mother saved for twenty years for a vacation in Bermuda. You don't know how hard—"

"Oh, knock it off." He pointed the light at Pam. "You."

"What?"

"What do you mean, *what?* What's your old man do?"

"Teacher."

"Teacher, teacher," Bogie mimicked. "What does he teach?"

"History at Clinton High."

"You got any brothers or sisters?"

"No."

"Where's your mother?"

"I don't want to talk about her!"

"Oooh, tiger cat," the man said. It was weird how benign he sounded, when only minutes ago he'd kicked me viciously. He flickered the light over Pam's face, then moved it deliberately down over her body. Up and down. My face heated up. Bastard!

He moved on to Ed.

"How about your old man, meatball?"

"He's a machinist," Ed said. "He's out of work now. He's been laid off since last fall."

"What about you, black boy?"

"My father's a grocer. Nights he's a guard in Wesley Iron Works. And my mother's a teacher in King Elementary."

"A bunch of working slobs," Bogie said. "I'm proud of you. Not a parasite among you, except for you-know-who, the one parasite here, the rich parasite."

"I'm not a parasite." Why did I bother answering him? I didn't have to defend myself, to him or to any of them.

"I say you are. All your life you've lived with a fence around you. A money fence. You got the Army and the Navy and the Air Force protecting you. Don't tell me you don't! I know! They work for your father. And in case they're not enough, there's the FBI, the police, and the Secret Service. You got them all working for you, parasite. Your father pays them off."

He ran his finger down his flattened nose. "I've been bashed plenty of times by the cops. When you're rich the cops bow and scrape, but when you're poor, pow, they break it off across your head like that." He cracked one hand against the wall. "What do you say to that, parasite? You got something smart to say now?"

I was silent. He was completely unpredictable. Crazy and mad . . . the way he'd killed Cocoa.

He turned to Ed. "When was the last time you saw a million bucks, meatball? Any of your fathers could work their tails off for the rest of their lives and they'd never see a million bucks. Not if they held down ten jobs and got themselves a case of the royal piles that wouldn't let them sit for a year."

He held up his hand and ticked off his fingers. "It takes three things to make it in this world. One! Money. Two! Brains. Three! Nerve. That's what I've got. Nerve. And Pearl's got the brains. And Chapman is going to give us the money."

"Right, right," Ed said. "So you don't need us, do you? We can't give you anything. We don't have any money. You could just let us go, just take us out of here, we don't know where we are. Take us down the road anywhere and leave us. We'd never say anything, man."

"Just take you down the road and let you go," Bogie repeated.

"That's right," Ed said eagerly. "You can trust us. No parasites, remember?"

"You think I'm stupid?"

"No, man!"

Bogie kicked an empty chair, knocking it over. "You think I'm stupid!" Behind the light, his face looked bloated, puffed up like a frog. "That Bogie is *stupid*, you must have been saying to yourself." He was breathing hard, pacing up and down. "That Bogie is stupid, they said. Stupid. That's what they said. Stupid Bogie! Is that it?" He swung around. "Is that it, Chapman?" He stepped toward me, his gun out. "Who's stupid?"

He pushed the gun in my face. I couldn't say a word. If I could have stopped breathing, I would have. I could smell the gun, feel its metallic chill in my bones.

Bogie was breathing raggedly. "Right now this gun is worth more than a million bucks. If I pull this trigger, all the money in the world couldn't help you."

The man *was* crazy. I could see the craziness in his eyes, smell it on him like sweat. I sat frozen, afraid to move.

The gun . . . you know . . . the thought of it exploding in my face . . . I was losing control of my body . . . everything running through me like water . . . I was terrified.

Then he laughed.

Looking straight at me, he laughed, enjoying my terror.

The sadist! *The son of a bitch!* It was a scream in my head. A scream of fury. That was the moment I found out about hate.

Maybe he saw it in my eyes, because he abruptly stuck the gun back in his belt and went downstairs.

"Hey, Chapman, you okay?" Jeff whispered from the end of the line.

"Okay." I really couldn't talk yet.

I was sweating. Couldn't catch my breath. And I wanted to cry, really bawl. But I didn't, not in front of the others. I felt so alone. So completely alone.

7

A few chinks of light came up through loose floor-boards. Downstairs, Bogie had turned on the radio. Someone was giving a weather report.

"I'd like to get out of here, man," Ed said.

"Why don't you ask your buddy, *man*," Jeff rumbled. "Captain Ghoul's a regular guy, everybody's friend. Maybe he'll let you go, *man*."

"Get off my back!"

"Not as long as you talk like a jackass."

"Look who's talking, fathead. I never met anybody who loves himself so much."

"How can you fight now?" Wendy whispered. "Everything's so terrible." She was crying.

"Don't!" Pam said. "You only make it worse for everybody. *Don't cry!*"

"I'll cry all I want to," Wendy choked. "Leave me alone."

"We've got to be strong—" Pam began.

"Oh, shut up, will you? Just be *quiet*. I'm not strong. I'm scared, I hate it here, I don't know *why* I'm here!"

After that for a long time there was only the sound of Wendy catching her breath and the music coming up faintly from downstairs. Every once in a while I'd catch a familiar phrase. I heard Arlo Guthrie twanging. *Good night, America, how are you?*

I dozed off. There was a snake with a blue belly crawling at my feet. The snake leaped, hung on my arm like a cat. I brushed it off, but it sprang again and bit me in the face. I couldn't get rid of it. Its teeth were sunk into my cheek . . .

I jerked awake. I was cold. It was pitch-black in the loft. Even the windows were black. What time was it? Was the woman talking to my father right now? Did he believe her? *Dad, she's telling the truth. I've been kidnapped. Dad, listen to her. You've got to get me free. Do what she says . . . Dad, can you hear me? Dad! Listen to me, Dad!*

"What's the matter, Derek?"

It was Pam, next to me. She was awake too. I could barely make out her face in the darkness. "Are you in pain?"

"No—why?"

"You were groaning."

I shook my head. "I'm all right. Pam—do you think people can communicate without talking?"

"Maybe."

"I was talking to my father, sending him a message about us. I believe in the sixth sense. Do you?"

"You mean ESP, foretelling the future? No, definitely not."

"Not just that, but communicating over distance, sending and receiving thoughts and emotions. Not feeling we're cut off from other people just because we're physically separated."

I really liked the way I sounded. I'd thought about ESP before, but I'd never talked to anyone about it. Not this way, smoothly, the words coming out so naturally. It took me by surprise. Maybe it was the darkness, or the incredible weird intimacy we'd been thrown into. Maybe it was being beaten up! I honestly didn't know what it was, just that suddenly I felt I could really talk. I was a real talker. *Smooth.* I was in love with the sound of my own voice.

"There've been times when I haven't heard from my mother or my sister for a while and I get worried. This one particular time, last year, I received this very strong feeling that something was wrong. I had to call up. I got out of bed about three o'clock in the morning to phone."

"Three o'clock in the morning!"

"Yeah, it was midnight in California. And I was right. Ora had been thrown by her horse that day and broken her arm."

"Just coincidence," Pam said. "What about all the times you worried and were wrong? What if your mother, for instance, really got sick and you never had any premonitions? What's *that?* What if she died?"

"Did your mother die?" I asked.

"Yes. Last year."

There was a long silence. A very long silence. Should

I speak? I *should* speak, I told myself, but what should I say? *Say you're sorry. That's what people say. Even if you never knew her mother, you are sorry. You're sorry she doesn't have a mother. That's awful. That's terrible. Say you're sorry.*

I should have said it right away. The longer I waited, the harder it got, the phonier I thought it would sound. It was too late. I couldn't say a word. That marvelous, miraculous looseness of speech was gone. All gone! I felt dumb, so dumb, almost inarticulate. Anything I said now would be the wrong thing.

"She died last year," Pam finally said. "Exactly nine months ago next week."

Say it. "I'm sorry."

"Thank you. I'm still not over it. None of us knew anything was wrong. She'd been feeling sort of tired— she thought it was going back to college and doing all the household stuff besides. Then she had this low-grade temp. Nothing much. They couldn't find anything wrong. She had tests, all these tests. And she said, 'Oh, let's just forget all this fussing, I'm fine, I'll be fine.' She wouldn't go to the doctor again. What for? she'd say. And we all forgot about it. Forgot anything was wrong. Then, suddenly, she was sick, very sick. Cancer. She was dying. Five weeks, that's all it took. She died."

She broke off abruptly. I barely remembered the fights my parents used to have. Mostly I remembered how terrible they made me feel. Once, I must have been small, there was a door—they were standing there, yelling at each other. My mother saying, "You're never here." My father saying something about business. I thought he said *big*-ness. I thought he meant himself. I was hugging his leg, solid leg, wool trousers, itchy, smelling of cigarettes. *Don't fight, please don't fight. I'll be good.* So scared he'd leave. And then it was Mom who left, taking Ora. Leaving me and Dad together. Like Pam and her father. Only for her, it was worse, much worse.

"Sorry," I whispered.

"Ahhh." She sighed, a long, sad sigh. Then she twisted as if she could burst out of the ropes by sheer will power. "I want to be free! I want to be away from these people."

"Pam. Shhh! He'll hear you. Listen," I said urgently, "my father is going to get us out of this. That woman is speaking to him right now, and he's saying okay about the money."

"You don't know that. You only wish it."

"I know it. I'm telling you, he isn't going to hold back. He's not like that. He'll get the money tomorrow—"

"Tomorrow? Tomorrow is Sunday."

"Sunday? Just Sunday? Are you sure?" It seemed impossible that not even twenty-four hours had passed. "Well, he'll get the money Monday, first thing, the moment the bank opens. He'll get the money for them and fly upstate. Monday afternoon, we'll be free."

"Another whole day and another night like this."

She groaned. "And then all day Monday. I can't bear it!"

"We ought to just take it hour by hour. Maybe that's the only way to get through this. Do you think so?"

"Hour by hour," she repeated. "You're right, I know you're right about that. Hour by hour. That's the way it was when my mother died. How many hours? Forty-eight? Forty-eight hours! That's so long!"

"Less," I said. "It must be near midnight now. Maybe it's Sunday already." I tried automatically to look at my wristwatch.

"Sunday, you think it's Sunday already?" She took a deep breath. "Let's say forty-three, forty-four hours," she said. "Now we've got our schedule, let's stick to it, troops."

"Yes, *sir*. Consider that an armless salute."

All the time we were whispering, I'd been inching my chair closer to hers. I got close enough to really see the pale oval of her face. "Pam, now I can see you. You're awfully pretty."

"So?"

"It's nice to look at someone good-looking."

"Is that all you think there is to me, Derek? There's more to me than that."

"I know that. You've got character, personality, intelligence—"

"Don't be slick!"

"I mean it sincerely. Maybe I'm not saying it just right. I feel that I really know you."

"I reject that idea. You don't know me. And as far as being a judge of character—if you had any judgment, you'd never have gotten into that van, or dragged me in after you."

I didn't answer. I felt totally put down. I'd almost forgotten how lousy I felt, but suddenly it was all there again, the aches, the soreness, the swelling in my face, the misery of being tied up.

I closed my eyes. I'd told Pam we'd be out of here by Monday, but maybe we'd never walk out alive. Maybe it would be easier for them to kill us all. *Bogie swinging Cocoa by the feet . . . smashing her into the tree . . .*

"Derek, listen, I'm sorry."

"You ought to be. You've got a mind of your own. You didn't have to get in that van!"

"You're right. I said I'm sorry. I was being mean. It's just—this is so bizarre, I hate not being able to move, and those people—" There was a catch in her voice. I thought she was crying.

"Anyway, I did get you into this. I followed you out of the lecture hall, I persuaded you to get in the van—"

"Let's not talk about that any more. My mother always told me, 'Don't cry over spilled milk.' Are you close to your parents, Derek?"

"Yeah. Not that we see that much of each other, but when we do it's good. How about you?"

"No more! My mother and I were really close, but I'm not close to my father any more."

"Why? What happened?"

"It hasn't even been a year since my mother died, and he's going with a woman. I don't talk to him. Just what's absolutely necessary."

"What's he going to think now? When you don't come home?"

"I don't care! Let him think I ran away. I thought he was a man of character, but now I know better."

"Pam, I like you very much. I know you think it's superficial, but these things can happen fast."

There was silence.

"Pam—"

"Derek—" At the same moment.

"ESP," I said.

"Just coincidence."

"You're a realist down to the core."

"And you're a romantic to the bone."

"Pam, do you have a boyfriend?"

"Many, my good man."

"Anyone special?"

"Not at the moment."

"Phew!"

"Do you have a girlfriend?" she said.

"Many, my good woman, but none at the present."

"Phew!"

We both laughed.

"Pam, let's make believe we're out on a date."

"What? In this romantic setting?"

"It's dark, anyway." I leaned over as far as I could. My face was close to her hair.

"Moonlight," she said, "coming through the floor. How perfect!"

"Guitars playing in the background." Bogie still had the radio on.

"What more could we want?" she said.

"So—let's make love," I said boldly. Our faces were very close. I stretched my neck, shoulders, head as far forward as the ropes would let me, smelled her hair, fresh shampoo smell, her skin smell. "Pam," I whispered, "turn your face a little . . ." Our lips brushed. It was strange for a moment, then we were pressing our mouths together as hard as we could. It was crazy, wonderful, I forgot everything—everything except the breathy softness of her lips. There was a marvelous sliding-swooping feeling inside me, like rolling down a grassy hill in the middle of summer.

We separated. "Hello," I said.

"Hello."

"You smiling?"

"Yes. You?"

"Yes! Pam, I feel happy. Is it stupid to feel so happy? Do you feel happy too? I want you to!"

We leaned toward each other again. She spoke against my lips. "Derek, I have both feelings. Happiness and unhappiness. Both. I forget where we are, and then I remember."

"Feel happy," I said. "When we get out of here, we'll really get to know each other. We'll talk."

"But it has to be honest."

"It will be. No secrets. No phony stuff."

"I like that," she said. "Do you really think we can tell each other the truth?"

"I know we can. This is the beginning. If we can be friends in a place like this, it has to be better outside." I felt lightheaded, as if I'd been drinking champagne at one of Mom's dinner parties. I rubbed my lips gently over hers, my nose against her nose. Nuzzling. Our necks stretched out like geese. I could have stayed that way forever.

Was it possible to be tied up, a prisoner, and still feel so good? "We must be crazy!" The other kids were sleeping. I could hear them moaning, muttering. I could have sung out a loud yell, a whoop, a song of my own. Hey, everyone, Pam Barbushek kissed me! Derek, you fool, you simple-minded fool.

"My neck is killing me," Pam whispered. "And your poor face!"

"I don't feel a thing! Better, all better!" We laughed and separated. I was half asleep, half awake, Pam's name in my mind. Pam Barbushek . . . Pam Barbushek . . . I liked the sound of it, the rhythm. I could feel myself getting excited. The idiot down there—I was grateful for the dark. I thought I was controlling myself, calling him down, but I was sleeping, that muzzy half sleep of exhaustion. I heard drums. Pounding . . .

I jerked awake, remembering half a dozen things at once: Cocoa's murder . . . the kiss . . . the gag in Wendy's mouth . . . the ropes . . . Pam . . . All jumbling together in my mind . . . a frantic feeling, my heart choking up into my throat, trying to hang on to the good thoughts of Pam, but the pounding . . . *Footsteps!* Footsteps pounding up the stairs. Then a light glaring into my eyes. A harsh voice. A burst of words. A slap in the face.

"Damn you!" Pearl. Another slap. My nose swelling. Blood coming into my mouth. "You listening to me? You gave me the wrong number, didn't you?"

The light was brutal in my eyes.

"Open your eyes! I'm talking to you. You want me to get Bogie up here?"

"What? What wrong number?"

"You know what I'm talking about. Your father's telephone number. I sat in that freaking phone booth for hours. *Hours*. The damn phone ringing, ringing, no answer, *no answer*—"

"I gave you the right number." My nose was throbbing. "Will you take that light out of my eyes, please?"

"Don't give me orders. Where is he?"

"I don't know. Home, I think. Maybe—he could be on a business trip."

"Where?"

I squeezed my eyes shut again. "Europe. Japan. South America. Lots of places."

"Doesn't he let you know?"

"Not always. He could be flying to Japan and be home before I even know it. If he's going for a long stay, like a month, he—"

"A *month*. Bogie! Bogie," she yelled, "get up here."

"A month," Ed echoed. Everyone was awake now. Someone groaned. Someone sneezed.

Bogie came in, his shirt unbuttoned.

"You hear that? This stupid kid says his stupid father goes out of the country for a month sometimes."

"He lets me know if he goes that long," I said quickly. "I don't think he's gone anywhere now." *Dad, didn't you hear me calling you? Dad, where are you? You should have been home, waiting for the call.* "He could have just been out, you know—" Staying over at Bryna's place, maybe.

"He got a girlfriend?" Bogie said.

"Yes."

"Just one?"

"Yes."

"What's her name? Where does she live? Her phone number?" Pearl rattled off the questions.

"Her name's Bryna. I don't know her number. She's an artist."

"Bryna what, stupid?"

I felt ashamed. I didn't know. She was part of Dad's private life. I'd met Bryna only a few times. A tall woman with hair down to the middle of her back. She hadn't said much to me.

"He'll be home tomorrow," I said. "I'm sure he'll be home tomorrow. He likes to spend Sundays at home." *Dad, be home.*

"Tomorrow," the woman said. "You better hope so,

because you and your friends are going to be sitting in those chairs till we get hold of the big man himself. You're going to be sitting there, just like you are now, if it takes us two weeks or two months. It's all the freakin' same to us."

8

Sunday morning. Still night in the loft, but in the diamond windows at the peak a gray light. A chill breeze inched in through the cracks in the walls. There was a dull ache in my jaw. My wrists and legs were numb. The others were sleeping, hidden in the gloom like dark mounds.

I looked bleakly out through the louver. The ice on the lake was cracking. I heard wind in the trees and birds singing.

Someone was moving around downstairs. The radio was on again. A door opened and closed.

I looked down the row at the others. Jeff's white sweater. Wendy, coughing repeatedly. I looked at Pam, remembering our kiss. Her braid had worked itself loose, and her hair partly covered her face.

"Pam," I whispered. Her eyes opened. "Hear the birds?"

She smiled.

"Did you sleep okay?"

"This way? Can you sleep sitting up?"

A door shut downstairs. "Maybe that's her going to phone my father."

Wendy heard us. "I sure hope she gets him today. I can't afford another night in this hotel."

"You call this a hotel?" Ed said, waking and yawning loudly. "This place stinks."

"Oh, I don't know how you can say that," Pam said. "I love it here."

Wendy was working her shoulders back and forth, then doing some kind of neck and jaw exercises. "You can have my accommodations any time."

"I'm ready to contribute mine, too," I said.

"What are you joking about, Chapman?" Ed said. "You should have dropped dead when you were born."

It was like a slap in the face. I looked away, swallowing a reply. Dumb little jerk! My whole mood changed just like that. A word could knock me down. I'd never been that way before.

"It's not Derek's fault we're here," Pam was saying.

"It's not my fault either," Ed said, "so what am I doing here, tied up like a hog?"

"You're being unfair . . ."

"Oh, dry up, you make me sick!"

"Look, creep, we're all in this together," Jeff said.

"Who you calling creep, you big bl—"

"*Shut up!*" Bogie yelled from below. And there was immediate silence.

After a while, Pam whispered, "Listen, everybody, we're all feeling rotten. But we've got to hold ourselves together. We can't fall apart and scream at each other all the time. It just makes things more awful."

"That's what I've been saying," Ed said. "Just co-operate and nobody will be hurt."

I looked at him in amazement. He was perfectly serious. Then Pam winked at me, and my mood switched again. Up I went. Why had I let Ed get under my skin?

Wendy suggested we play games to make the time pass, or tell stories, keep each other entertained. Right away Ed said, "Let Derek entertain us. It's his party."

"I don't have any ice cream and cake," I said, "but I want to say that if I could do anything to set you all free this instant, I would."

"Anything?" Ed said.

"Yes."

"How about turning all your money over to me?"

"If it would get us free, sure."

"You liar! How much do you have?" he said.

"Nothing of my own now, but when I'm twenty-one I get a trust fund my father set up for me."

"How much? Give it to me in dollars and cents."

"I don't know exactly." I didn't like all this talk about money. If it were up to me, I'd never mention money again. What was the big deal about money? Sure, we had it, but so what?

"Come on, you know how much that trust fund is. You rich people are always counting your money. Is it a million?"

"Something like that," I said reluctantly.

"Do you hear that! A million bucks. What a liar. You wouldn't give it away, Chapman. You're like your old man. He's probably still squeezing the first dollar he ever made. The rich don't give away anything, man."

"I would," I said childishly, stung again. "Anything, if it would get us out of here."

"Easy to say. You guys believe him?"

Silence. Not even Pam looked at me. Was that what they all believed? That because I was rich I was greedy and stingy?

Then Jeff said, "Derek can't help it that he was born rich." He paused. "Some people just don't have *any* luck." His timing and the way he drawled out "any" was perfect. It broke the tension.

"Listen, everyone," Wendy said. "It's Sunday morning, and I've been thinking about what we have for breakfast at home. Who wants to hear? We have French toast slathered with butter and maple syrup—"

"Wait a minute, wait a minute," Ed said, "don't go so fast. Real maple syrup?"

"No, that's too sweet. *And* expensive. We buy a quart of the real stuff, Vermont maple syrup, in the fall at the farmers' market, and then we mix it with the syrup we buy in the supermarket. Okay? It's really good. We always have a big pot of cocoa, too, with our French toast." Wendy wet her lips. "We just stuff ourselves every Sunday morning. You know those little tiny sausages? We fry them up, a big panful, till they're almost black—"

"I didn't know you Jews ate sausage," Ed said. "That's pig."

"We do, we're not kosher. Mmmm, I can just taste them now."

"Me too," Ed said.

"Oooh, my stomach—"

You'd think that, being so hungry, we wouldn't want to hear about eating, but we all wanted to talk about food.

Jeff described in detail the cheese omelettes that his father made. "He puts in mushrooms, green peppers, and scallions all chopped up fine. He cooks it in sweet butter. That's important, not margarine, but real sweet butter, and—"

"That's nothing," Ed butted in. "*My* father makes us all the pancakes you can eat for Sunday breakfast. My mother and my sister go to church, and my father fixes everything for when they come home. Talk about stuffing yourself! You wouldn't even be able to walk away from our table. Don't tell me about *real*. In June we always have big bowls of fresh strawberries, none of that frozen junk, with real fresh cream. Mom and my sister, Lynn, pick our own strawberries at Hafner's farm, about fifty quarts. Mom makes strawberry jam, and we have strawberry shortcake about three times a week, and strawberry sherbet, and strawberry chiffon pie. Everything with real sweet cream. We chill it in the refrigerator with the bowl and the beater. Then we whip it up. Oh, man, it's beautiful, all thick and wavy."

We were all groaning, but we didn't want him to stop. Wendy rolled her eyes. "Oooh, this is killing me. The first thing I'm going to do when I get home is drink half a gallon of milk, cold, ice-cold milk."

"I'm going to climb in our refrigerator and not come out for a week," Jeff said.

"And I'm going to climb in the tub and soak for a week," Pam said.

"I'll climb in with you," Ed said.

"What's that supposed to be," Pam said, "a joke?"

"Don't you think it's funny?"

"No."

"Don't you have a sense of humor?"

"Try saying something funny."

"Okay. Here's a joke. Knock, knock."

"Who's there?" Wendy said.

"Diamond."

"Diamond who?"

"Diamond the mood for love."

We all hissed and booed.

"Don't you get it?" Ed said. "Di-mond the mood for love. Di—"

"We get it, we get it!"

"Boo! Hiss!"

"Hit him with a rotten egg," Jeff said.

"Never mind, Ed," Wendy said, "I like it. I like

jokes like that. Do you know how the little moron showed he had guts?"

"No, how?"

"I don't want to know!"

"He jumped off the Empire State Building."

"Aaaggghh!"

"Wendy, you're as bad as Ed."

"Worse!"

"Okay," Ed said, "knock, knock."

"Who's there?" Wendy obliged.

"Marmalade."

"Marmalade who?"

"That's what Poppa wants to know."

"Oooh, dirty!"

"Nasty!"

"*Fun*-ny."

In the midst of our laughter, there was a pounding on the floor from below, and then the footsteps.

"Watch out," Jeff whispered. "Here comes the animal."

My ears buzzed. I had told myself I wasn't going to let fear rule me, but I tensed up when Bogie entered the room. His eyes looked small, morning mean, and he looked at me first.

Without saying a word, he untied Ed and poked him down the stairs. The bathroom routine. One by one he took us all down and then up, saving me again for last, the flushing detail. After he tied me up again, he left. No food! None of us had had anything to eat or drink for nearly twenty-four hours.

Pam was the first one to start calling. "Water, please, we want water!" Then we all joined in.

"Give us something to eat."

"Hey, can you hear us? Food. We want food."

"*We want food!*"

Yelling was exhilarating—we were doing something—but it lasted for only a moment. Then Bogie was charging up the stairs. "Shut your mouths! Or I'll gag all of you." His jowls quivered. "You kids shut up! Just shut up!" Glaring at us.

There was a long heavy silence, with only the sound of breathing. Then Pam ventured, "Look, we really need a drink, and—"

"I know all about it, mouthie!"

"You going to give us something?" she persisted.

"When I get good and ready, and not before. So shut up."

About an hour later he came back upstairs with a carton of milk, a loaf of bread, and a hunk of bologna under his arm. He untied Wendy and told her to feed us. I couldn't take my eyes off the milk carton. I was that dry. I swallowed and swallowed again. I could taste the milk sliding down my throat. Bogie pulled out a chair and sat down. He had the gun and a brown paper bag in his lap. He pointed to Jeff. "Start at that end of the line. Leave the parasite for last." He took a banana out of the bag and peeled it.

Wendy tipped the milk carton to Jeff's lips. Some of it spilled. I groaned. Ed was next. One sip and he twisted his head away. "It's sour!"

"Drink it anyway," Wendy said. "It's good for you, Eddie."

After Pam, Wendy, and then it was my turn at the milk. It *was* sour, but it was liquid and food. I was going to eat anything offered. The bread was okay, but the bologna was overspiced. Pam complained, "This is going to make us thirstier than ever."

"You got something to say about everything, don't you, blondie," Bogie said. He was eating a round raspberry tart, the juice spilling from the corner of his mouth. "This isn't a restaurant." He looked into the paper bag. Out came another raspberry tart. "You know what?" he said, with his mouth full. He pointed to Pam. "You got a big mouth, but you're cute. Very, very cute." His eyes were on her breasts. "I like big girls."

Pam's face got red. I stared furiously at the man. Slimy pig! I was so filled with anger that for a moment I heard the voices outside without registering what I was hearing. ". . . Isn't this great! What a view." Then, in that second, when it came to me— *there were people outside*—Bogie moved. He grabbed Wendy around the neck and stuck the gun against her breast. "All of you, *still! Don't move.*" The veins on his temples bulged.

I tipped my head, barely moving, and slanted my eyes down through the louver. I caught a glimpse of a man in a red plaid jacket and a boy wearing a dark sweater.

We're here! Up here! Look up here. Help!

". . . must have walked ten miles," the boy was saying, his voice so clear that he might have been standing next to me in the attic.

The man laughed. "Don't exaggerate. Just two and a half, Barry. You're just not used to walking."

The van—they must have seen it. Were they blind, or just stupid? Then I remembered that Pearl had gone out again. But what about tire tracks? Wouldn't they show on the road?

"Isn't it great here?" the man was saying. "Isn't nature beautiful?"

"Come on, Dad—"

"Not a soul around. Listen to the quiet!"

If he'd only shut up he'd hear the sounds of our breathing. *Listen . . . listen . . . listen . . . !* My whole body flushed hot with hope. *Listen, we're up here!*

"It's just like I told you, Barry. These summer people don't appreciate what they have. All this beauty, and they let these places sit here empty most of the year."

I moved my head another fraction of an inch. The man was looking out at the lake. The boy was slouched against the tree. The same tree that Bogie had smashed Cocoa against. Surely they'd see Cocoa's body. Again that hot swift flush of hope poured over me. Maybe that was why Cocoa had died—so her body would lead to our rescue. For a second I believed that. Believed it as surely and as deeply as if I were six years old, not sixteen. Then that little flicker of hope burned out too. Would Bogie be so stupid as to leave the dog's body around for someone to discover? He must have buried her, or at least thrown the corpse into the woods for the animals to clean up.

"Do we have to walk all the way back?" the boy said. He was staring up at the lodge—staring up at me. How could he be so blind!

"Look up there, Barry." The man raised his binoculars. My heart leaped. "Right over the roof, there— there. See it?" He was pointing his binoculars straight toward the louver. Didn't he see me? Couldn't he see that I was tied up, a prisoner? *Look at me. Look . . . look!*

"It's a hawk, Barry. A red tail. See it?"

"I saw it. It's a bird. Okay? Can we go now? My feet are freezing."

"Freezing! Mine are burning."

"Mine are freezing, Dad."

"You should have worn wool socks. I told you, didn't I . . ."

Their voices were growing distant.

". . . all the way around the lake? Dad, are you kidding! You're unreal. I don't want to walk all that way."

". . . do you good . . ."

Their voices faded. They were gone.

Gone. I couldn't believe it.

They were coming back. They had to come back.

Come back! Come back!

Tears of frustration filled my eyes. Then a rush of sour fury filled my throat. Those stupid people. Those stupid, stupid people! I spit the sourness out, spit on the floor.

"Hey! What the frig are you doing? That's disgusting." Sweat dripped off Bogie. He loosened his grip on Wendy, pushed her roughly into her chair, and lashed her up. There were red marks on her neck. He went down the row and one by one gagged each of us.

9

All day Sunday Bogie left us tied and gagged. Sleep was the best way to make the time pass, the best way to forget where I was. But I couldn't sleep for very long. My head would drop to my chest, lower and lower; then suddenly I'd jerk awake, groaning and struggling against the ropes.

I remembered a book I'd read about a woman in a Russian prison who'd been thrown into solitary confinement for ten months, and how she kept herself from going crazy by disciplining herself to use her mind every single day. After a while she was able to remember millions of things she'd learned years before and thought she'd forgotten. That was what I should do: discipline my mind. I was falling behind in Latin in school, and I had a paper due for English in three days that I hadn't even started. I could write the paper mentally, then repeat it to myself enough times so I'd remember it word for word when I got back. Then I'd just sit down and write it out without a stop. I actually tried to do that, but I couldn't make

my mind stay on the subject long enough. I kept drift-
ing off. It was just about impossible to think of anything except how miserable, crummy, rotten I felt.

I heard Bogie moving around downstairs. Five steps
down. Then five steps back. Up and back . . . up and
back . . . Hour after hour.

Several times he came upstairs to check us. He
tightened the ropes and the gags. Then he left.

The day seemed to go on forever. It was horrible.
We couldn't talk to each other. We couldn't quarrel.
We couldn't do anything. The worst of it were the
fantasies that crowded my mind. Being left here . . .
never found . . . starving to death in this attic . . . Did
anyone even know I was missing? Greenie. Wouldn't
he report it when I didn't return Saturday night?
Maybe. Maybe not. If he did, the school must have
tried to reach my father. But I wasn't even sure of
that. Maybe they'd wait, hoping I'd come in, not wanting Dad to find out they didn't know where his son
was every minute.

When darkness finally came, I thought: Now he'll
take off the gags, at least, because nobody's going to
come here at night. I waited for him to come up.
Closed my eyes. Counted. Hundred and one . . . hundred and two . . . hundred and three . . .

But he didn't come near us again.

The dark made time pass even more slowly.

At least in the light I had been able to look at Pam.
I could look out the louver. I could look at the stuff
in the attic. Now—nothing. Darkness in front of my

eyes. And darkness in my head. I told myself: When morning comes, it'll be better.

I smelled bacon frying, coffee. I thought I smelled it. Maybe I just wanted to smell it. It was the most wonderful smell I'd ever smelled. I sniffed hungrily, as if the smell of food could nourish me. He was eating downstairs. Stuffing his face. He wasn't going to go hungry.

Much later I heard a faint hum in the distance. Slowly it got louder, became more distinct. Came closer. It was a car. A car was coming. *A car was coming down this road.*

I straightened up as far as the ropes let me. The bird watchers! They had seen something after all. They hadn't let on. All that talk—Aw, Dad, it's just a bird, the boy had said—But it had been a signal. He'd seen me. He'd been too smart to blurt it out. As soon as they were out of sight, he'd told his father. They'd doubled around, gone back to their car, then straight to the police. The thing would sound farfetched at first. *You were looking through binoculars and you saw a boy tied up in an attic? Yes, sir, that's exactly what I saw* ... The boy wouldn't let them shake him. He wouldn't give up till they came back here with him.

The car motor cut off.

Silence.

Had I really heard the motor? Or only wanted to hear it, the way I'd wanted to smell bacon and coffee?

I listened.

I heard wind rustling in the trees.

I heard one of the others groaning.

Something pattered on the roof.

Then footsteps on the ground outside.

My scalp prickled. Someone was creeping up to the lodge. Had Bogie heard them? Was he listening too? Where had they come from? Then I realized they'd hidden the car up the road. Of course. They weren't about to announce their presence. They intended to take him by surprise.

I heard Bogie shuffling around below. I felt a puff of air. The door downstairs had opened. In a flash, I saw it all. Police. Guns drawn. *Hands on top of your head. One wrong move, and—where are they? We know you have the Chapman boy—*

"Didn't you hear me whistle? I almost broke my neck coming through the dark." It was Pearl downstairs. I'd imagined the whole thing. It was Pearl who had driven down the road. Pearl who had hidden the van.

Idiot! I berated myself viciously for grasping at straws. Dreamer! Stupid! You think you help yourself having these juvenile daydreams? Hands on top of your head. Cops and robbers. Good guys and bad guys. *No one is coming.*

Pearl was talking fast. She'd lowered her voice. I was agitated and couldn't catch a word. Had she reached my father? What if she hadn't? The thought of spending another day bound and gagged made me wild to be free. I started twisting and fighting the ropes. All these hours immobilized. I had to move my arms and legs. Nobody could stay still this long! It was inhuman.

I made so much noise that Bogie came running upstairs. "Who's making that racket?"

I grunted in my throat. He flashed the light full in my face. "What's your trouble, Chapman? You asking for a fist in your face?"

I kept grunting and scraping my chair. *Did Pearl reach my father? Answer me!* I was mad with frustration.

"If you don't quit that, I'm gonna nail your feet to the floor!"

Pam's head swung toward me. Her eyes were big, reflecting the light. She shook her head back and forth, warning me.

I subsided.

I was trembling.

Bogie went downstairs.

Darkness again. Pam's face remained like a picture before my eyes, that quick vivid glimpse I'd had: her hair, her dark eyebrows, the small, full mouth. I tried to hold on to that, to breathe evenly and deeply. When morning comes, I told myself repeatedly, it will be better.

I was awake long before dawn. I saw the first light edge in through the louver. I saw Pam wake up. Almost at the same moment, I heard Bogie's steps on the stairs. His heavy tread. He untied Jeff from the chair and prodded him out, down the stairs. I heard the door open, then close. Through the louver, I caught a glimpse of Bogie shoving Jeff along the path, down toward the water.

Pearl came up and took Ed away.

Then Bogie was back, untying Pam. Rough. Big, meaty hands all over her. I was alarmed; everything about the man alarmed me: his sullen look, the way he was manhandling Pam. Stop it. Leave her alone. I tried to warn him with my eyes. Then he shoved her out the door, like the others still gagged, hands tied behind her back.

Only Wendy and I were left. Bogie plodded back up the stairs. He took Wendy away. I was alone. Where were they taking everyone? Why had they left me for last?

Outside, someone screamed. Screamed again.

Pam?

Wendy.

Screams. Again and again. Deep-throated, awful, so awful, so full of misery I wanted to bite through the ropes. *It was Wendy. What are they doing to you? Wendy! Pam!* I could hardly bear it. I wrenched against the ropes.

Abruptly the screams stopped.

Footsteps scraped along the path. "Everything okay?" Pearl called.

"They're all in, locked up solid."

They were standing in the same spot where the man and his son had stood. "You hear the kid screaming?" Bogie wiped his forehead disgustedly. "That dumb redhead saw her mutt in the boathouse. Started screaming like I'd knifed her mother. I thought they'd hear her clear across the lake. I shut her up fast. Booted her good in the tail. Stupid little shit."

"Forget it. Let's get the goods and go."

He came up for me and untied me. I hung back, hot with hate. He pushed me down the stairs and out the door. It was the first time I'd been outside in two days. The sky was gray. Mist hung in the pines. At the edge of the lake there was a small fieldstone building—the boathouse. I looked up at the lodge: bark siding, a wide fieldstone chimney jutting up at one end. I wanted to remember everything—for afterward.

"What are you looking at?" Bogie shoved me. But not toward the boathouse. I held back. He pushed me again, toward the van, which was parked near the lodge. "Move, jackass." He punched me in the small of the back and rushed me into the van.

They left the door between the cab and the back open. Bogie drove. Pearl sat half twisted around to face me, her gun in her lap.

The van jounced over the dirt road. "I still say it's stupid," he said.

She half turned. "I told you, Bogie, I *had* to do it. He said, 'I want proof my son's alive.' He said he had to hear Derek or no deal. And no tape recordings. Derek right on the phone. So what was I supposed to do?"

"We're just giving him more time to get the cops."

"He's not going to do that. I told him," she said in a chilling voice, "he does anything like that, he gets the kid back piece by piece in Band-Aid boxes."

I shifted so I could look past her through the windshield to see if I could recognize anything on the road. There were just trees and bushes on both sides.

"Get back in the corner," she ordered.

They drove for a long time after they turned off the dirt road. The first time they stopped, only she got out. She was gone a few minutes, and then she was back and we were driving again.

I thought about Pam . . . Wendy. Frustration and rage jammed my throat.

They stopped again. Again Pearl got out. "You get him?" Bogie asked when she came back.

"I got him. I got him hanging by his nails."

"What'd he say?"

"I didn't give him a chance to say anything. I told him, 'You're going to be talking to your son sometime today, but after that no more calls till tomorrow.' Then I told him, 'You better be at the Airport Inn tomorrow afternoon with the money. That's all the time we're giving you. And no police, no FBI. Or your kid's dead. It's all the same to us.'"

"What'd he say to that?"

"'I want to talk to my son.' Bleating like a goat. 'Where's my son?' I told him to stay by the phone, and I hung up."

They drove for a long time. I didn't want to listen to them. I was a prisoner, but my mind was free. *Die gedanken sind frei . . . my thoughts are free.* Where had that come from? Think, Derek, someone taught you that . . . a girl . . . yes . . . okay, got it. Gene Ellis! Two summers ago. Tennis camp. You were supposed to be there to improve your game. Ha, ha, big joke of the summer on the boys' side. *You improve your game last night? Don't ask!* Gene. First time I ever saw a girl completely undressed. First time. Only time. Last time?

Die gedanken sind frei . . . that was a German song from way back in the 1930s, from concentration camps . . . one of Gene's songs. *Let all tyrants tremble . . . though I'm a prisoner . . . my mind is free . . .* Something like that. *Die gedanken sind frei!* My mind is free. Thank you, Gene . . . keep thinking, Derek. Get away from them with your mind. Think about Pam. You can think about anything you want. Pam . . . a hot dusty road . . . the two of us on bikes . . . we'll stop under a tree . . . we'll eat sandwiches and talk . . . then we'll lie down, our arms around each other, kissing . . . kissing . . . and—

"Derek. Derek! Wake up! You listening to me?" Pearl yelled. The van had stopped. I hated her voice.

"We're going to take off your gag. Then you're going on the phone. Fast. And you're getting off fast. You say hello to your father, how are you, I'm fine, and that's it. Understand?"

She untied the gag. I spit it out and worked my jaws. My tongue felt swollen. She got out, and the man motioned me forward. She was in a glass-enclosed phone booth by the side of the road. She had the receiver to her ear. He crowded me into the phone booth with her. She shoved the receiver against my ear. I could hear the phone ringing in our apartment.

My father had phones beside his bed on the side table where he kept his papers and magazines, white phones. A red phone was in an alcove in the hall. The one in the kitchen on the counter next to the juice extractor was yellow. In my room there was an old-fashioned standing phone with a separate earpiece. They were all ringing. Five phones ringing at the same time.

Then my father was on the line. "Hello!"

Hearing his voice, I choked up.

"Hello? Hello!"

Pearl jabbed me in the kidneys. "Dad," I got out. I swallowed hard.

"Derek? Is that you, Derek? Are you all right? Are you all right, Derek?"

"Dad—" I was in tears, trembling.

"Derek? Derek! What is it? Have they hurt you? What have they done to you? Derek—"

"Dad—"

She jabbed me again. "Say something!"

"They mean it, Dad." I couldn't hold my voice steady. "Do what they say. They've got guns, Dad. They've got five of—"

The phone connection went dead. Pearl had cut us off.

"Why'd you do that?" I shouted. "Dad! Dad! I want to talk to my father!"

She yanked the phone out of my hand and shoved me out of the booth. A car sped past. A scream formed in my throat. "Don't you dare," she said. I felt the gun grinding against my ribs. "Get in the van."

I stumbled and let myself fall. I didn't want to get in the van again. I didn't want to be gagged again. I wanted to be free. Not just my thoughts, my body, too!

"Dammit, I never saw anyone so clumsy!"

Bogie hauled me up. He twisted my arm behind my back, making me gasp with pain. "Smartass," he said. "Get in."

Like a beaten dog, I crawled into the van and let myself be locked in again.

10

After they had me talk to my father, Bogie and Pearl drove around for hours, calling Dad from different phone booths, never stopping at any one place for more than a couple of minutes. They wanted half a million dollars in small unmarked bills, packed in two black plastic garbage bags. I had a brief vision of Dad hauling two stuffed garbage bags onto the plane. The steward would try to take the bag away from him, but he wouldn't be parted from them. He'd buy two extra first-class seats, one for each of his garbage-bag pals.

It was nearly dark again when Bogie and Pearl drove back to the lodge. They parked the van in the woods; then Pearl went down the road to the lodge to make sure no one was around. She whistled to him as an all-clear signal. Then, while he went for the others, in the boathouse, she took me inside. A fast stop at the toilet, then upstairs again, into the chair, the ropes knotted swiftly. The others were brought up, one at a time. In minutes we were all tied up again.

"I talked to my father," I whispered to the others. They were still gagged. Ed, Jeff, and Pam all turned toward me intently, listening. But Wendy sat like a zombie, not looking at anyone or anything, her eyes dull and unfocused.

Bogie and Pearl came upstairs. They ungagged the others. They had food for us. They shoved bread into our mouths, a piece of American cheese, a hunk of bologna. I chewed and swallowed, nearly choking on the food. They went down the line and spilled soda into our mouths. Barely enough to slake my thirst.

"More. I want more," Pam said. She was tied up at the other end of the line from me.

"I'll give you more. I'll give you back that gag," Pearl said. She stared at Pam. Pam didn't answer. Pearl and Bogie went downstairs.

"I hate those people," Pam whispered fiercely. "All day with that filthy rag in my mouth. In the dark, tied up. I hate them."

"Someday I'll get them back," Jeff said. "I thought about that today. That's all I thought about. Getting them back."

I told about all the phone calls they'd made, how they'd hardly let me talk to Dad. "But he's going to get moving now," I said. "He won't waste any time."

"Did your father definitely hear you?" Ed asked. "Are you sure he heard you? Or did she cut you off too fast?"

"He heard me."

"Did he know it was you?"

"Yes."

"How can you be sure? Maybe he thought it was them pretending to be you."

"Don't be an ass," Jeff said. "You can't just imitate someone else's voice unless you have a talent for it. Voices are like fingerprints—everyone is different."

"Then if he knew it was you, he's coming with the money, right? He's coming tomorrow, right?" Ed said. "He gives them the money and they let us free, right?"

"Right, right, right," Jeff said. "Everything according to plan."

His sarcasm didn't faze Ed. "Wendy, you hear that? Wendy? We're going to be free tomorrow, so cheer up. Okay?"

Wendy didn't answer.

"You'll get another dog," Ed said.

"Don't," Pam said.

"Well, she will. Her parents will buy her another one."

"Maybe she doesn't want another one."

"That's one thing you can always get," Ed said, "another dog. One year our bitch had a litter of ten. We had to drown half of them."

"Shut up!" Pam said. "Wendy loved Cocoa. Another dog can't take her place. You ever lose someone you love? If you didn't, just shut up about things you don't know anything about."

"I'm going to sleep," Jeff said. "I'm tuning out. I've had it. Wake me in the morning, somebody."

After that, no one said anything. It was a long

night. I wanted terribly to talk to Pam, but she was too far away. After a while I fell asleep.

I woke up, my heart beating painfully. I'd been dreaming. I was on my way to a class. Late. There was a knot in my chest. I kept going up the wrong staircase. What a snob! someone said. I tried to explain. *Listen, how we are born is immaterial, it's important to distinguish . . .* I knew I was only making things worse. I kept explaining. *No matter who our parents are, we are . . . we are . . .* I woke up.

Dawn. Gray light filtering into the attic. I heard them moving downstairs. A thick depression settled over me. I closed my eyes. I wanted to sleep. Forget.

"On your feet!" Bogie and Pearl rushed into the room, shining lights in our faces, yanking our ropes loose, pushing us down the stairs in a confused herd. They ordered us to use the bathroom, hurrying us every moment. They tied us up again and pushed us outside, into the raw, chilly dawn. "Move!" They were like dogs snapping at our heels. They ran us toward the stone boathouse.

"No," Wendy moaned. "No."

In the boathouse, water lapped at the edges of the boat slip. Above it, a motor launch hung suspended by chains. And in the corner was Cocoa's body.

"No, no, no, no," Wendy whimpered.

They moved us into the windowless stone room in back. The heavy wooden door swung shut. A bolt slid into place. Footsteps on the decking. A crunch of feet on the path above us, going away.

It was dank. Cold. Black. Not a glimmer of light. Wendy's moans escalated. "Cocoa . . . Cocoa . . . Cocoa . . ."

"Don't cry, Wendy," Ed said. "Where are you? Don't cry."

"Cry all you want," Pam said.

Someone bumped into me. I couldn't see.

"Go on, Wendy, cry," Pam said. "Just lean on me and cry." Sobs burst from Wendy, great wrenching sobs that made me feel like crying myself.

"I'm not staying here!" Jeff shouted. "One day in this pit was enough. Hey, you white assholes, let me out! You hear me? *Let me out!*"

"Cripes, shut up!" Ed exclaimed. "Keep yelling like that and you'll start a race riot. We just have to wait a few more hours, right? The deal is, they get the money and then they let us go, right? You sure your father's coming today with the money, Derek? What'd he say on the phone?"

"He didn't have a chance to say anything. I told you, she cut me right off."

"You mean he isn't coming!"

"I didn't say that! She told him to be there with the money, so I assume he will be—"

"What do you mean, you *assume*—is he coming or isn't he?"

"How does Derek know?" Pam said. "He doesn't know any more than you do. He told you—"

"You're always taking his side, big mouth!"

"Don't talk to her that way," I said.

"You going to stop me?"

"If I could see you in this dark—"

"I'm right here!" Suddenly he butted into me and knocked me back. I butted back blindly. It was ridiculous, both of us with our hands tied. But I was furious.

It ended as swiftly as it had started. In the dark, Jeff managed to get between us. "You're both a couple of jerks! Save your strength."

What strength? That little explosion had left me weak and trembling. I leaned against the damp wall. Then I felt Pam next to me, her lips against my cheek. "You okay?" she whispered.

A moment later we heard them outside. Ed got all excited, saying they'd come back to release us after all. "I told you so!" At first, when the hammering started, no one understood what was happening. We crowded around the door, waiting to be released.

"What are they doing?" Ed said. "What are you doing?"

"What's the hammering?"

Bang! Bang! Bang!

"They're driving nails into the door," Ed said disbelievingly.

"They're nailing us in," Pam said. Then she screamed.

In the dark, we ran into each other, kicking the door, screaming.

"Don't! Let us out!"

"Please . . . don't nail us in, oh, please, please . . ."

Then we fell silent at last. There was nothing to

hear but our own ragged breathing, and the faint sound of water lapping at the dock.

"Oh, Christ, oh, hell, oh, hell, oh, hell, oh, god, get me out of here." Jeff's voice cracked.

A terrible heat rushed through me. It was awful: the darkness, being in the dark, being nailed in, sealed into this stone cell. I pressed against the door. Somebody was crying. "They're coming back," Ed kept saying in a high voice. "They're coming back for us."

"No!" Pam's voice rose above the others. "Once they have the money, why should they come back? It would be dangerous and stupid, from their point of view. They'll never come back."

There was a stunned silence. "You're crazy! They can't leave us here," Wendy said.

"Once they get that money, they're going to run as far and as fast as they can," Pam insisted.

"They could tell someone else to come get us."

"Why should they?"

"Because—because they can't leave us here. They just can't."

"Yes they can," Pam went on. "They're capable of anything. *You* should know that. We've seen them, every one of us has seen both of them up close. I could draw you their faces with my eyes closed. Don't you understand, we could identify them. They must have police records. If they let us free, where would we go? Straight to the police. They know that—they're not that stupid."

Pam was right. They weren't coming back. All the

talk about being freed—dreams! And now what? Day after day in this room, without food or water. Growing weaker and weaker. We would die here. I kicked the door, kicked it again, kicked it as hard as I could.

There was a long, terrible silence.

"Got to get out," Jeff mumbled next to me. "Got to get out. Got to. Got to get my hands free."

All this time I hadn't even thought to try to free myself from the ropes. It was the shock of being nailed in. But, also, it proved how fast I—all of us—had been conditioned to being prisoners, tied up and shoved around like cattle.

I hated the way I'd surrendered and let myself become a prisoner. That was the way I'd lived my whole life. Things happened to me and I just accepted them. Mr. Happy-go-lucky himself. I tore one wrist against the other, trying to shake the ropes loose. I hated myself for every minute, every second I'd let myself accept the prisoner psychology. For every shove they'd given me, every crack and blow. I should have tried harder! I should have been smarter, stronger, braver. I was desperate to be free. I *would* be free.

Jeff backed up against me. "Is that you, Derek? What are you doing? Take it easy! You can't free yourself alone. Here—I'll work on your ropes, and you work on mine."

Back to back, we worked at each other's ropes. My fingers were stiff and swollen. I fumbled clumsily at the knots, frustrated at not being able to use both hands together. I could only pick at his knots with one hand. It was a long, slow, painful process. Ed and Wendy worked back to back. Ed kept up a steady stream of talk.

"Once I get my hands free, I'll free everyone else. Then we'll find a way out of here. There's got to be a way out. You ever hear of a room you couldn't get out of it, somehow? No way are they going to keep me locked up here. What do you say, Wendy? You agree? Anyway, it's better than yesterday, right? Anything's got to be better than yesterday. Couldn't speak, couldn't do anything. At least today we can talk, right?"

Every time Ed fell silent, there was nothing to hear but our own heavy breathing. *Keep talking.* I didn't want to talk. All I wanted was to be free.

Ed was free first. Wendy untied him, then he untied her, and they freed the rest of us.

With our hands freed, our spirits rose. Even the dark didn't seem quite so dark now that I could explore a little. I ran my hands along one wall, then another, digging my nails into the mortar between the fieldstones, trying to find a loose stone. The others were exploring too. We were like five moles, sniffing around, bumping into each other, mumbling to ourselves.

Wendy found a table with a big moldy canvas on top, and Pam found a couple of oars in a corner. Jeff climbed up on the table, probing for a loose board in the ceiling with one of the oars. "Anything?" I asked hopefully.

"Nothing."

We searched the room, inch by inch. We tried everything, even bashing the cement floor with the oars. We were nailed in solid as a rock.

Then Ed ordered us all out of the way. "I'm going straight through that door. Look out! *Aaaagh!* My shoulder! Oh, man, that door is solid."

We all tried to hit it together, but there were too many of us. All we were doing was knocking into each other in the dark.

"At the count of three," Ed said, and then Jeff, Ed, and I, the three heaviest, raced for the door together. I bruised my shoulder, caught an elbow in the shoulder. The door didn't budge.

"There's still a chance someone will come," Wendy said.

"When?" Jeff said. "In June? That's three months. They'll find five skeletons."

"Don't talk that way," Pam said. "It's demoralizing."

"I don't believe in fairy tales except on a stage," Jeff said. "If we don't get out of here, you know that what I'm saying is the exact truth. We're going to die. One by one, the weakest first. I don't know how fast it'll happen, but it's going to happen."

"Shut up with that talk!" Ed yelled. "You're scaring the girls."

"Scaring you, you mean. Well, you listen and be scared, little big man, because a skeleton is a skeleton is a skeleton. Skeletons have no color but bone color, and one dead body stinks like another!"

I found Jeff and dug my fingers into his arm. "What's the use of that?"

He shook me off. "Listen, I've heard my grandmother tell stories about her grandmother, who was a slave. I heard those stories when I was a little kid, and I listened and I thought about what I was hearing, and that's when I knew that you don't tell yourself fairy tales in life. If you're black, you're black, and if you're locked in a grave, you're locked in a grave. Pretending isn't going to make it any other way."

"Shhh!" Wendy said. "I hear something."

We all listened.

Little scratchy sounds.

Someone was at the door.

Then we were all on our feet, yelling and pounding on the door. "Help! . . . We're in here . . . Get us out!"

But when we stopped and listened, we heard nothing—just the lap of water against the dock.

Then the scratching sound started again.

"It's nobody," Ed said. "Nothing! It's an animal, a dumb stupid animal. Get away from here!" he raged.

There was a tightness in my chest, a hard lump of misery working itself from my throat down to my stomach. I slumped down on the floor, wrapping my arms around my knees.

"Let's try to sleep," Wendy whispered, as if the darkness had stolen her voice.

Someone groaned. There were coughs and whispers. The damp crept into my bones.

"We ought to sleep in shifts," Pam said. "Someone has to stay awake in case anyone does come. It might happen, Jeff, being realistic doesn't mean a thing can't happen."

"I'm going to nod off too," he said. "You stay alert, Wonder Woman."

Pam sat down next to me. I touched her arm. She'd lost her yellow slicker. I couldn't remember when it had happened. The last thing I thought was, Her skin is so soft ... feels so good ...

I don't know how long I slept. Half a dozen times I woke and stared into the darkness. Was I awake or asleep? Images and fantasies filled my mind. I heard a truck rumbling toward me. Was I hearing things or dreaming?

"Do you hear it?" I said.

"What?" asked Pam.

"Listen!"

Nothing. The wind had come up; that was all.

Pam put her arms around me. We held each other. We kissed. We whispered to each other. I felt myself growing excited. The idiot again. I couldn't help myself. Despite everything I felt happy. I even thought: Without them, would this ever have been? For a long time it was mostly quiet. Then Wendy jerked up, yelling, "Here, we're in here!" She thought she'd heard something. We all yelled.

But it was the same as before. Nothing had changed. There was only the wind in the trees, and the splash of water against the dock. At times the wind was almost like the wake of a motorboat splashing on the shore, but in the end it was nothing again.

"What time is it?" Wendy said into the darkness.

"Late. The middle of the night."

"It's tomorrow."

"Tomorrow? Really? You really think so?"

Hours passed. I felt cold, shivery. I wasn't hungry, but every once in a while a wave of lightheadedness passed over me.

I must have slept again. A shout woke me. I sat up, feeling confused and anxious. How long had I slept? It was dark when I fell asleep, and dark when I woke. Did they know we were here? Had the bird watchers returned, the man and his son? "We're in here," I yelled. "Here!"

"What's the matter with you?" Jeff said from across the room. "What are you yelling about?"

"I heard something, a shout—"

"It was me, you moron. You heard me," he said with a whoop of delight, "I just found a book of matches in this table."

11

A light flickered into the darkness.

I saw Jeff's face. He held a match between his fingers. I looked from one shadowy face to the other. How disconnected the darkness had made me feel. How wonderful it was to see everyone.

The match flickered out. We moaned almost in unison.

"Light another one," I said.

"No," Pam said. "Save them!"

"Maybe we can burn one of the ropes," Ed said. "No, give me an oar, I got a better idea. I got a terrific idea. Just give me a second. I'm going to split this oar into a million pieces."

"What for? What are you doing?" Wendy said. "Don't break the oar."

We heard the oar crack. "What do you want to save it for? You going to row away from here? Light another match," he ordered. He held a piece of the oar, just a thin sliver of wood, to the flame. The dry hardwood caught almost instantly, giving off a long narrow yellow light. He threw the oarlocks to one side.

We spread the canvas on the floor, and Jeff, holding the taper carefully, sat cross-legged in the middle. We all crowded around him.

"I love light," Wendy said. "I'll never sleep in the dark again."

"Oh, light, light, precious light," Pam said, bending forward as if she were praying.

"Out, out, brief candle," Jeff said dramatically.

"No!"

"Don't say that."

"Don't breathe so hard, everybody. Look at the way the flame quivers when we talk."

We sat quietly around the lighted splinter. Up and down. I was on a seesaw of despair and hope. Despite the fact that nothing had changed, I was almost happy.

"Now, if someone would just come for us," Wendy said.

"Who would you like it to be?" Jeff said. "Bogie and Pearl?"

"Anybody but those Nazis!"

After the first taper burned down, we lit another one. For a long time we talked, feverish, excited, anxious talk. We went over everything. What were the kidnappers doing now? Had they met my father? Did they have the money? Would they let someone know where we were? Would they really leave us here? Where were we, anyway?

Opinions were offered on everything, but none of us knew anything. The only thing we did know for sure was that we were nailed into this stone room, and we couldn't count on anybody coming to let us out.

We broke up and tried everything we'd tried before: digging at the stones, ramming into the door, poking at the ceiling. Nothing worked.

The second taper burned lower. Pam and Jeff got into an argument about lighting another one. Pam insisted we could burn everything, because we were going to get out.

"How?" Jeff said.

"Somehow."

"You were the one who wanted to save the matches before," Jeff said.

"Well, now I don't! We can't get out of here if we can't see what we're doing."

"We're not doing anything."

"I don't care. I've got to have light. I'm not going to molder in that filthy darkness again." There was an edge to her voice I hadn't heard before. "I'm getting out!" She jumped up, every muscle, every tendon taut. "I thought you felt the same way."

"You think you're the only one," he said. "But blabbing isn't going to spring us. We've got to think about this. Use your intelligence, Pamela."

"Don't patronize me," she cried. " 'Use your intelligence, Pamela,' " she mimicked. "Use yours, Jefferson!" I tugged at Pam's hand, trying to pull her down.

She jerked away. "Leave me alone! How can you all just sit here and do nothing? God!" Her lips strained back over her teeth. She pounded on the door.

"Hey, come on." I patted her shoulder and put my arm around her. She was trembling uncontrollably. I didn't know what to do. "Come on, Pam, don't, you're just hurting yourself." I was really shook up by her outburst. We'd all blown one time or another, but Pam had been so steady.

The taper flickered out. We were in the dark again.

"Put that light on!" Pam cried. "Put it on, dammit!"

Ed lit another taper. "There's your light," Ed said. "All you have to do is snap your fingers, lady, and you get anything you want."

"Sure. Thanks." Pam slid down on the canvas next to Wendy and put her head down on her arms.

"You feeling okay now, Wonder Woman?" Jeff said.

"Sure," she said dully.

"Hey, we're going to find a way out," Wendy said. "Listen, Pam, you know we are—you're the one who's said it all along."

"Sure," Pam said again, as if she didn't believe a word of it, didn't believe anything any more. It was the worst thing, seeing Pam like that. It shook up everyone.

"I'd like to burn this freakin' place down," Ed said.

"Brilliant," Jeff said.

"Lay off him," I said. "He's just talking. We all feel crummy. Anyway, maybe he's got something—"

"Sure he does. Rocks in his head."

"No, I mean it. What if we started a small fire, controlled it, burned down that damn door!"

"That's stupid!"

"Not the whole door," I said. "Just a hole right through the door. Then we could widen it with the oarlocks, chop it out. Who's for that idea?"

"Fire's dangerous," Wendy said.

"What's our choice?" I yelled. "Wait? Trust those two sadists? I say, let's burn our way out of here! Who's for burning through the door. What do you say, Pam?"

"I don't know, I have to think about it—"

"There's nothing to think about, it's crazy," Jeff said.

"You're crazy," Ed broke in. "I think Derek has hit on it. The fire's going to get us out of here."

"Says who?"

"No way are we going to make a fire in here."

"Will you listen to me!"

For a while we were all yelling back and forth, arguing till we were hoarse; then we started all over again, till we couldn't talk any more. Right from the start it was Ed and me against Jeff. Every objection he raised we had an answer for. Wendy and Pam were the swing votes. But the idea that we could free ourselves was irresistible. "Let's do it," Wendy said at last. Jeff still held out. We all badgered him, till finally he said, "Okay! Okay, I'll go with it, but we're going to be careful. I mean *cautious*."

"Right, right, we're going to be very careful," Ed said. "Let's get the wood, let's get going. Come on, Derek."

"Keep the canvas near the door," Pam said. She had picked it up as we talked. She was herself again. "We'll throw it over the fire if it starts getting too big."

We went to work, getting the wood together first. Ed splintered the remaining oar. Jeff and I, the two tallest, stood on the table and pulled down long splinters from the rough ceiling joists.

Wendy knelt by the door and made a little wigwam. "This is the way we did it in the Girl Scouts." She tore off the matchbook cover and tucked it carefully under the wigwam. "Taper, please!" She lit the matchbook cover. It flared up. The splinters caught. The fire rose in a bright yellow column. We crouched around it. Sparks flew. A little smoke drifted upward and hung under the ceiling. "Tilt it toward the door," Ed said, blowing the flames down gently. The door began to char.

It was really exciting. We took turns tending the fire and chopping at the charred spot with the oarlocks. Despite our excitement, we were all desperately tired and weak from lack of food. No one did anything for very long. It was slow going. Gradually, though, a shallow depression began to form.

It was the enameled table leg that started the trouble. We needed more wood. The oars had been burned. Ed and I knocked the table apart, but when we put the first leg in the fire, black, acrid fumes spurted up. The paint was smoldering.

Wendy started coughing. "Get it out of there!" Pam darted forward and kicked the table leg into a corner. It continued smoldering, giving off thick fumes. We were all coughing. We threw the canvas over the leg, but that made things worse. The canvas began to char. Heavy, choking fumes filled the room. It was impossible to breathe.

"Put it out!" Ed cried. "My eyes are killing me!"

"I can't breathe!"

"Oh, it's horrible, stop it, put it out!"

Coughing and choking, our eyes tearing, we stamped on the canvas. The fire, untended, leaped up along the door, lighting up the room. Jeff shouted and began swatting at the flames with his hands.

"The canvas!" Pam exclaimed. "Use the canvas!" She and I grabbed it and dragged it toward the fire. Ed pulled off his shirt. We were all yelling.

"The room is on fire!"

"Put it out! Oh, god, put it out!"

Flames darted up the door, reaching for the ceiling beams. Sparks showered down. I smelled burning hair. The room filled with smoke. I couldn't see anything. I crouched over. The heat . . . my skin . . . I was blinded. I couldn't breathe. My *lungs*. It was a furnace. I was at the door, an oarlock in my fist, punching frenziedly. I was crying, mad with fear.

Screaming, "Open, open, open, open."

12

Hacking blindly at the door.

Smoke ... fire ... strangled cries.

Fire in my lungs.

"Open, open, open, open . . ." The harsh, crazy sound of my own voice. Of all the ways there were to die, this was the worst. Better to be shot, wiped out in a car, drowned . . . Oh, yes! To be underwater now, filling my scalded lungs with water, cool water. Refreshing water over me, still, cool water . . . dead, but cool ... so wonderfully cool ...

I drove my fist feebly into the wall. I was all done ... couldn't breathe . . . couldn't move . . . strength all gone ...

Next to me, Jeff sobbed harshly.

Pam, where are you? We didn't get to talk. I'm sorry ... so sorry ...

The door was no longer in front of me. I could go through it. I was breathing again, fresh, cool air. *I'm dead*, I thought dazedly. *I've died*. I never dreamed it would be this sweet, this real. I crawled forward.

There was a light coming toward me from a great distance, a glowing, shimmering light. And fresh air. Greedily I sucked in cool lungfuls.

Then hands grabbed me. Not gentle, angelic hands. Real hands, rough, hurting, yanking me forward by the hair.

"Stupid, stupid, idiot kids!" The ghouls were back. It was Bogie's voice, Bogie's hands. I was dragged along the decking . . . Dropped.

Choking, coughing, I pulled myself to hands and knees. Jeff fell against me, his hands over his eyes. Behind us smoke poured out of the room.

"We've got him, let's go," Pearl said. "Take the other one, too."

They dragged us to our feet and pushed us out of the boathouse. They pulled the door shut.

It was night. "The others—" I said. They pushed us toward the lodge. The van was waiting.

"No, the others—" I tried to turn back. Didn't they understand?

Bogie flung us toward the van. "Move, both of you. In the van."

I stumbled forward, then broke free. *Get Pam . . . Get Wendy . . . Ed . . .* I don't remember running. I felt nothing . . . no pain, no fear . . . just running. Jeff was behind me . . . Pearl and Bogie shouting. I plunged into the boathouse. Blinding smoke was everywhere. I couldn't breathe. I dropped to the floor . . . touched an arm . . . wiry hair . . . Wendy. I dragged her out.

Jeff found Ed. Together we pulled him out. "Pam," I gasped. Jeff and I started back. We found her crawling blindly. We dragged her forward.

We were all out. Sparks flew up from the roof, lighting up the trees. Wendy bent over, vomiting. Tears streamed from Jeff's eyes.

"In the van, in the van!" Bogie yelled. He booted Ed to his feet, yanked Pam up by an arm, dragged them both toward the van. Pearl had Wendy. "Get Derek!" she yelled.

Run . . . Get up, Derek, move . . . It's only a step, and you'll be in the woods.

In my mind I was there already, but by the time I pulled myself up, Bogie had me. They locked us all in the van, then sped away.

I slumped on the floor next to Pam. I smelled fire and smoke. "You okay?" I asked.

"Okay," she said, coughing.

I was parched, alternately hot and then chilled. My eyes were swollen. Wendy was coughing. We were all coughing, but talking, too.

"I don't know how I got out," Ed said. "I thought it was all over. I don't know how I was saved. God must have saved me."

"Jeff and Derek saved you," Pam said. "They pulled the three of us out."

"We almost died," Wendy said in a wondering voice. "I could be dead right now. I was almost burned up. But I'm alive. We're all alive."

None of us could stop talking.

"I didn't feel anything," Jeff said. "I just kept going. I didn't even know how much my eyes hurt till now."

"Your eyes? What happened to your eyes?"

"They're bad, really bad. I can't see anything. It's so dark in here."

"It's dark because there's no light," Ed said. "And because it's night."

"No, it's darker than that. There's something really wrong with my eyes. They're burning. I burned them! They hurt too much. I can't keep them open."

"Derek," Pam whispered to me, "one of us has to do something. Jeff needs a doctor. We have to get away from these people. They're going to kill us."

Up front, Pearl and Bogie were talking in loud, angry voices that carried over the whine of the motor.

"You did something wrong," he was saying. "Why wouldn't Chapman be there? Everything's going haywire. You must have called the wrong motel."

"The Airport Inn. I called the Airport Inn. There's only one Airport Inn. I called it. I called it six times! You heard me telling him to be there. I told him. The Airport Inn. What is he, stupid?"

"Then why wasn't he there if you told him? Tell me that. Why wasn't he there?"

"How should I know why he wasn't there?" Pearl said. "You heard me talking to the SOB yesterday. I told him, soon as your plane comes in, you get a room at the Airport Inn. You sit there and wait for our call. Don't go out of that room."

"And what did he say?"

"He said yes to everything. Yes, yes, yes."

"He's double-crossing us," Bogie said.

"No," Pearl said vehemently. "Something happened to delay him. He isn't pulling anything as long as we've got the goods. The kid's still solid gold. Half a mill, Bogie. Don't forget it. Half a freakin' million! In a couple hours I start calling his father again. At the Airport Inn. He'll be there."

"He better be. And he better have a freakin' good reason why he wasn't there before," Bogie said. "That rich moron! That stupid jackass. Does he think we're playing tiddlywinks?"

Ed shook my arm. "Derek, your father never came with the money. Is he trying to kill us all?"

"Maybe he missed his plane," Wendy said.

"He's coming! Dad won't let me down." God. How could I believe anything else. He was coming through. Something had happened to hold him up. An accident, maybe. What if he'd had a heart attack or a stroke from the tension. My heart seemed to tighten unbearably. *Dad, come on. Dad, I'm counting on you.*

"Now they've got to wait for your father," Ed said. "So they've got to keep riding around with us till they talk to him again, right? You know what I think? I think they were going to leave us all to burn up in the boathouse. They want to get rid of us. They don't care about us. They just wanted to save Derek."

And then, as if to confirm Ed's statement, Bogie said, "Dead weight. That's what those stinking kids are. Nothing but dead weight. Carting them around like this—hell! It's stupid."

The monotonous whine of the tires kept me half asleep. Each time my eyes closed, I saw the flames racing across the cabin joists.

Off and on I heard Bogie and Pearl. Once they stopped and changed places behind the wheel. They drove around for hours. I thought I was talking to my mother. Then Ora was singing . . . flames . . . I was so hot . . .

A shot brought me awake.

I sat up, my heart pounding. The van bumped to a halt. They'd shot somebody! "Pam—Ed—"

"They're stuck," Wendy said. "They just blew out a tire."

Doors slammed. Bogie and Pearl were outside. "I told you it was a flat." He kicked the van.

"Take it easy, we've had flats before. Let's get it changed and get going again."

The hubcap clattered to the ground. "All day the same freakin' trouble. Every freakin' thing has been going wrong. It's those freakin' kids."

Quietly, without speaking, we had all stepped to the sliding door to the cab. The same thought had occurred to each of us. The cab was empty.

Pam tried the handle. Locked.

"Let me," Ed whispered. "I'll break it." He tried: then the two of us jerked down on the handle. The noise brought Pearl running. She unlocked the sliding door. "What are you kids doing? Down! All of you, down on the floor." She pointed a gun at us. "Face down on the floor. Hands behind your back!"

The others fell down. I stood there. What if I refused? Would she shoot me? They needed me alive. Did she even have real bullets in that gun?

I stepped toward her. *You won't shoot me. I'm solid gold. Remember?*

Hero stuff. For a second I saw it all. The gun wavering in her hand. Stepping coolly around her . . . leaping to the ground . . . running . . .

She pointed the gun at my head. Her hand was completely steady. "Get down there with your friends, Derek. *Down, I say.*"

Outside there was a grunt as Bogie jacked up the rear end. A car sped past on the road.

"Not a whisper," Pearl ordered.

I lay on the floor with the others, praying for someone to come along. Another driver. No, a state trooper, big, aggressive, suspicious of the van so late at night. He'd ask to see Bogie's license. Jeff and I would rush Pearl. No, not Jeff; I'd forgotten about his eyes. It would have to be Ed, Pam, and me. We'd rush Pearl. Take the gun. Yell. Bogie would make a run for it. The trooper would shoot. I saw the blood spurting out of Bogie's back. He'd die in the middle of the road. How I prayed for that trooper with his gun.

Another car sped past. Then there was a different sound—a car slowing down.

"*Quiet.*" Pearl shifted tensely over us.

The car stopped. Light seeped into the van. I nearly stopped breathing.

"Need some help?" a man's voice slurred. "Always glad to help someone in trouble."

"Thanks, buddy, but I'm all done." Bogie was tightening the lugs now. "Kill that light, will you, buddy?"

"Hey. Sorry. Just trying to be helpful to a pal."

"Just bug off, then!"

"Bug off? I'm doing you a favor, you creep."

"Bug off, I said, before I call the cops on you."

Bogie jumped into the cab and sent the van spinning onto the highway.

Pearl moved back into the cab. She locked the door. Nothing had changed.

Then Bogie said, "I've got it. I know where we dump them." He swung the van sharply around.

"Derek—" Pam leaned against me, her lips to my ear. "I'm going to get away."

I thought it was just talk. We'd all been saying the same thing since the beginning.

"Derek, when it's all over—" She kissed me swiftly. She got up and banged on the door connecting to the cab. I tried to pull her down.

She pushed my hand away. "Never mind, Derek, I know what I'm doing." She hit the door. "Stop, please! Please! I've got to go, it'll only take a moment. *Listen,* I can't stand it." She made her voice piteous. "Really! *Please . . .*"

The van slowed, jounced off the main road, and a few minutes later stopped. Pearl opened the back door. It was dawn. A faint pale light showed along the edge of the sky. Pearl pointed to Pam. "Let's go. Fast."

Pam hopped off the back of the van. Her hair hung loose around her face. She stopped, looking around. Pearl pushed her. Pam turned again, smiling at me. Inside me, something contracted into a hard tight knot of fear. "Wait—" I said. Pearl slammed and locked the door.

A minute passed. No more than a minute. Then a shot. Another shot. Then silence.

Then running feet.

I couldn't catch my breath.

"Pam," I whispered.

The cab door slammed. "*Go*," Pearl said. "The dumb kid tried to run. I had to—"

"What?" he said.

"Go. Get *out* of here!"

The van lurched forward. I shook the door handles. "Pam!" I slammed my fists into the door. "Pam! Pam!"

13

They ran us through a woods. Bogie in front, Pearl behind. We were in a line, roped together at the waist, hands tied behind our backs. We kept running into one another, stumbling and falling. We were all in a state of shock. They could have done anything to us just then, marched us off the top of a cliff, and we would have gone without a word of protest.

They'd shot Pam.

Killed her.

Each time I thought it, numbness engulfed me.

Wendy turned. "Derek—" Her eyes were sunken, her skin stretched taught against the bones. "Derek—" She appealed to me, as if I could tell her what we all knew wasn't so.

It was damp and slippery in the woods. Snow lay in patches at the edge of rocks and under trees. They goaded us on like a couple of lunatics. Jeff slipped and went down on his knees. He had a rag covering his eyes. Bogie kicked him to his feet.

Spurts of feeling passed through my mind. Desperate thoughts. I stared at the back of Bogie's neck, a thick, stupid neck. I wanted to put my hands around his neck and choke the breath out of him. I imagined kicking him in the stomach, the groin, the mouth, every vulnerable place on his body. I'd kick and kick, grind his face into the ground. Then, with a start, I realized that it was Pearl who had killed Pam, not Bogie. I twisted around to look at her. Her hair was disordered, blowing around her face. It was nearly as light as Pam's hair. She was chewing gum, her jaws working steadily. She didn't look like a murderer. She looked mindless. That's what they both were: mind-less and brutal.

I staggered blindly forward.

Pam, Pam, Pam, Pam . . .

They drove us steadily uphill for fifteen or twenty minutes. We slowed down only to splash across a rocky stream. We were all gasping for breath.

We came out into a clearing. Off to one side was a little weathered cabin, boarded up tight. Rising be-hind it was the bolted steelwork of a fire tower. In the early-morning light, it seemed as grim as the watch-tower of a penitentiary.

I looked around for a way to run. Woods all around us. I started toward the cabin, imagining someone crouched behind one of the boarded windows, watch-ing through a tiny peephole. If I could slip away, behind the cabin . . . but how? We were all bound together.

A blow on my neck snapped me forward. They

herded us to the foot of the tower. The huge steel feet were bolted to bare rock. We started up the narrow, open, crisscrossing stairs. We were still tied together. Jeff blindly raised one foot after another. The tower swayed under our weight. If one of us slipped, we'd all fall. Only a thin metal railing stood between us and the ground.

Through the openings between the stairs, I saw the ground receding, then the tops of trees. Halfway up, Ed collapsed in a heap, jerking the rest of us to a halt, forcing us against the metal railing.

"Heights make me sick," Ed moaned. "I can't go up there."

"Get up, you little coward." Bogie grabbed him.

"I can't. I'm dizzy. I'm going to fall. Everything's going round and round!"

Bogie dragged him up the stairs by one arm.

An overhead trapdoor led to the observation tower. It was chained and locked. Sweating like a pig, Bogie shook the lock, then pulled out his gun. A deafening crack followed. He knocked the shattered lock aside. He heaved up the door and disappeared into the tower. "Get them up here," he called from above.

In the dusty square room they pushed us down on the floor. A wooden bench ran along three walls. There was a glass map case. A telephone sat on the floor. Pearl lifted the receiver. "Dead," she said with satisfaction.

Bogie ripped the wires out of the wall, then with the butt of his gun smashed the map case and crumpled the map into his coat pocket. He checked his gun. He turned toward me. Our eyes met. I felt his hatred like a force in the air between us. He kicked me. "Your father better be there!"

They checked our ropes, then went out, banging down the trapdoor. The chains rattled as they knotted them again and again.

Their footsteps receded, then disappeared. We were still alive, but there was no rejoicing. Too much had happened. The fire ... Jeff's blindness ... Pam ...

Pam. I couldn't stop thinking about her. She should have been here with us. I heard the shots again. Pam. One shot. Another. I saw her lying on the ground. The whole scene unreeling in my head as if I'd witnessed it ...

Pam walking into the trees ... looking back at Pearl ... looking for a way to run. Knowing she was going to run. Was she frightened? Yes. But brave. Determined. Outraged. More that than frightened. Did she think Pearl wouldn't pull the trigger? Wonder Woman. Did she think she could outrun bullets?

Had she waited till she had a tree between her and Pearl? *I need a little privacy,* she must have said, and stepped behind a tree. Then run. Run for her life. For our lives.

Pam. I remembered the way I'd seen her the first time, coming out of the lecture hall. How I'd followed her and talked her into getting into the van. I saw her face, her hair uncombed, those fearless eyes.

There was a harsh, tight, terrible feeling in my chest. Somewhere in those tree-covered hills Pam was lying on the ground, dead.

I dozed off, head down on my chest, then woke with a start. Ed was groaning, sicker than ever, as the tower swayed under a lashing wind.

Time passed; it was impossible to say how much. We sat where they'd left us, numb, depressed, each locked in his own thoughts. The sky thickened with gray, heavy clouds. A storm was coming fast.

A bird flew against the window. The room darkened. Lightning cracked across the sky. Then the rumble of thunder. I jerked involuntarily against the ropes. "Uhhh-uhhh," Ed moaned. Rain spattered on the roof, smeared the windows. I licked my lips. I was parched.

For hours we had said almost nothing to each other. The storm—the lightning, the rain pelting the tower —revived us. Behind me, Wendy's hands touched mine. Without speaking, we fumbled at the ropes around each other's wrists.

Knot by knot we slowly freed ourselves, then helped Jeff and Ed. We were all in terrible shape, shivering and then burning, but Ed and Jeff were really bad. Above his stained white sweater, Jeff's face was badly blistered. He could see shadows, he said, lifting the rag, but it was misery for him to keep his eyes open.

I moved from window to window. Eleven windows, every one sealed shut.

The trapdoor could be raised a couple of inches. Wendy and I yanked it up and down as hard as we could, but the chains held.

Trapped, I thought. Trapped again.

I paced the square room, looking down through the windows on each side. I saw the tops of trees, the sheer drop down the tower. Puddles of water glistened on the bare rocks below.

Pam . . . I saw the rain falling on her, glistening in her hair, saw her lying face down on the ground . . . Was she like me, did she love the rain? I'd never asked her. She lay there now indifferent to everything.

Wendy paced back and forth like a nervous cat. Jeff moved slowly around the room, hands outstretched, as if he were practicing to be a blind man. Only Ed sat still, holding himself around the middle. "Stop moving," Ed groaned. "You're making me dizzy. You're making the room shake."

It was the wind, rattling at the windows, swaying the tower like a reed. Ed was green around the mouth. "I'm going to be sick," he said, and it happened. Yellow bile spurted from his mouth over his shoes and the floor.

In that sealed, damp room, the stench was overpowering.

"Who did that?" Jeff said. "Ed? Where is it? Get me away from it."

I took his arm, and we all moved as far away from Ed as possible.

"Ugh," Wendy said, "I can't stand this."

"Sorry," Ed said miserably.

"Oh, it's not your fault," Wendy said.

"It's not?" Jeff said. "Whose is it? Mine? Why did he have to puke right in our faces?"

Wendy took off her cardigan and mopped up the vomit with it, her face screwed up against the smell.

"It still stinks," Jeff said.

Wendy gave him a mean look, then pulled off her shoe and flung it through a window, shattering it.

"Hey, what's that?" Jeff yelled.

Wendy dropped her fouled sweater out the opening. Fresh air flooded the room. She and I helped Ed to the window, but looking out made him feel queasier than ever. He retreated, leaving the three of us crowded together, breathing in the clean, rain-washed air.

"How far up are we?" Jeff said.

"High," I said.

"How high is that?" he said irritably. "Ten feet? Twenty feet? Fifty feet?"

"Higher than that."

Below us was the spreading network of metal that supported the tower, then the tops of trees rolling away into the distance. I thought it looked like a huge green carpet. Just step out! Freedom was that close, and yet completely out of our grasp. If only I could step out the window and walk away, just walk over the tops of the trees.

14

"Hel-loooo . . ."
"Hel-loooo . . ."
My voice echoed through the hills.

The storm had ended. The sun shone narrowly from the western sky. I stood at the window, breaking out the remaining shards of glass.

"Hel-loooo . . ." I called again, then listened. I heard nothing but the echo of my own voice, a lonely sound filling me with the most desolate thoughts.

No one knew we were here except Bogie and Pearl. My eyes followed the path they had taken past the foot of the tower, past the cabin, then along the slab of rock to where the path entered the woods going down the hill. They'd return the same way, coming up the hill and out of the woods.

Was it possible they'd come back? My father hadn't shown up once. What if he didn't show this time either? No, he would. He'd move mountains to get here. He knew the danger I was in. My father was one hundred percent reliable. But a nagging fear kept working on me. Something had already gone wrong. Dad had missed the first time. Why? An accident? Yes, or worse than that. Heart attack.

I pushed the thought away but it came back. Dad was one of those hard-driving types. Type A's, the doctors called them, heart-attack prone. I could see him in the hospital, unable to speak. No one would know about me. Bogie and Pearl would think he'd double-crossed them. They'd be crazy with rage, hating us all worse than ever. They had started killing with Pam. Nothing would stop them now.

"What if they come back?" I said.

Jeff raised his head. "Did you hear something? Are they out there?"

"No," I said. I looked down fearfully. They could be coming any minute.

"We won't let them in," Wendy said. She was sitting next to Ed, knotting together the ropes we'd been tied with. "We'll stand on the trapdoor."

"A lot of good that will do," Jeff exclaimed. He felt his way to the trapdoor, and started yanking on it so violently he should have torn it off. If only he had! But he only wore himself down. He paced back and forth, back and forth. "You tell me the minute you see them. Keep watching out the window! You hear me?" he raged. "I'm not going to be caught off guard."

Wendy held up the ropes, which she had tied together into a single long strand. "Derek, let's see how far this will reach. If it reaches, you could tie one end around my waist and let me down to the ground."

I dropped the rope out the window. What she was proposing didn't register at first, and then it didn't matter anyway. The rope didn't even reach halfway to the ground. I pulled it up and dropped it on the floor. "Not even close."

Wendy bit her lip. "I thought it was too short. I just couldn't help hoping—"

"Don't hope, think," Jeff snapped. "You're not Batman, you're not even Wonder Woman. You're just a dumb little kid in the same stinking mess as the rest of us."

Wendy flushed and kicked the coiled rope. "You don't have to be so nasty. Just because you hurt your eyes."

"Don't talk until the shoe fits. How do you think I feel? You ever hear of a blind actor? A blind anything? Blind black men sell pencils on street corners!"

"All right, all right, I'm sorry!" Wendy yelled. "But I don't take back what I said."

Jeff whirled around. "Sorry doesn't mean shit. Get me out of here! Derek, you hear me? You hear me, Chapman? Where are you? You got me into this, you get me out of it. I need a doctor. I need attention for my eyes. Chapman, are you listening? Are you paying attention? *Get me out of here!*"

"Who do you think I am, God?" I yelled back. "You tell me how to get out of this place and I'll do it." I was ready to brawl over anything, but just then I noticed Wendy leaning out the window. Leaning so far out that her feet were actually off the floor.

"What do you think you're doing?" I grabbed her belt. "You crazy?"

"Hey! Let go."

"Get back in here," I ordered, holding her by the belt.

"When I'm good and ready. Will you let go? I'm thinking of something important. *Let go!*"

"No!" The crazy kid. We were all cracking up. I hung on to her belt till she pulled back in.

"I know how we can get out of here," she said.

"Another one of your brilliant ideas?" I said.

She shook my arm. "Shut up and listen! What we have to do is tie the rope around my waist and let me out the window—"

"No!"

"*Listen!* You'll let me down on the rope about ten or twelve feet, that's all. I don't have to go all the way to the ground. I just have to get a good swing going, swing out and then back in through the iron struts. I'll grab on to one of the struts and climb over to the stairs and untie those chains."

I leaned out the window. Sensible? Not exactly! Mad? Definitely. She wanted to swing like a ball at the end of a string, out and back, sixty, maybe eighty feet in the air. And said it as calmly as if she were talking about walking through an unlocked door.

"Forget it, Wendy. It's a stupid idea. There's no gym mat down there."

"What are you talking about? I'm not afraid of heights. I work on the high bar all the time. I have excellent control of my body."

I knelt down and examined the trapdoor again. "I don't hear you, Wendy." There were three oversize strap hinges on the door. If I could unscrew them— "Anybody have a penknife?" I said it before I remembered that none of us had anything any more, except the clothes on our backs.

"Derek," Wendy said in a loud voice, "come over here. You hear me! You listen to me! Don't be thick-headed. My idea is not stupid."

"Then it's dangerous and ridiculous. Okay?"

"I told you, I'm a gymnast. I can do these things. We'll be careful. What's the matter with you? Don't you want to get out of here? I can't do this alone. You have to work with me." Her lips jutted stubbornly. "Well? Will you do it? Will you?"

"What are you two talking about?" Ed raised his head. "Who's going out the window? Wendy, you're not going to do anything so crazy! Aaaagh—" He gagged. "Just the thought of it makes me sick." He staggered to his feet. "Derek, if you let her do that I'll kill you. Wendy, you listen to me—"

Wendy's face reddened. "All of you, stop treating me like a child. I've figured out how we can break out of here, and all you guys are too chicken to go with it. You all make me sick." She kicked off her other shoe.

"If anybody does it, I should," I said.

"Baloney, Derek. Have you ever done anything like this? No one's asking you to go out there. I'm ready to do it, but I need your help."

I looked down the side of the tower. Steel all the way down to rock. There was a shivery feeling in my wrists. If we did it . . . if the ropes didn't hold . . .

"We'll tie one end of the rope around my waist," she said, "the other around a leg of the bench. And then you let me down, Derek. You know it's the only way out of this place."

It was true. I thought of Pam. Then of Bogie and Pearl. Where was my father now? Was anyone looking for us? My hands were sweating. The sun was low. We'd been here all day. Too long.

"You know we can't stay here," Wendy pleaded. "You said it yourself. They could come back any moment. I don't want to be here when they come back! I'm ready to go *right now*."

It was up to me. Nobody else. Ed was too sick to be objective. Jeff couldn't see enough to really assess the situation. If I said no, Wendy would have to stay. If I said yes, she'd go. And if anything happened, it would be my fault.

I swallowed hard, wiping my palms on my pants. I'd never had to make a decision like that in my life before, where someone else's life would actually depend on what I said and what I did.

I looked out the window again, thinking about the rope breaking.

Yes or no?

No meant she was safe. But for how long? If Bogie and Pearl returned, none of us would be safe.

"Okay," I said finally, wetting my lips. "I'll help you."

My hands were still sweating as I wound the rope around Wendy's waist. I tested the knots by standing on the bench and lifting her off the floor. Then I anchored the loose end of the rope around the bench leg, but I didn't like that. Wood could crack. The leg might buckle under the pressure of Wendy's weight.

"I'll be her anchor," Jeff said. "I'll be good for something." I tied the rope around his waist. I checked and double-checked each knot.

Ed tried to argue Wendy out of it again. "Wendy, don't let them make you do this." He'd lost his glasses. It made him look so bare, actually vulnerable. He came up close, peering into her face pleadingly. It was dumb of me not to have realized till then how he felt about her.

"It's okay, Eddie," she said. "Trust me. I'm not scared."

She sat on the sill, her legs dangling. She looked pale and serious. We all fell silent. I think we were all gripped by the same fear and hope. I had a feeling that if we pulled through, this would be a moment we wouldn't forget.

"I'm ready," Wendy said.

I let the rope out inch by inch.

I watched her go down, as if I could keep her safe by never taking my eyes off her. Only once I looked past her to the ground. I didn't let myself do that again.

When she was about ten feet down she called me to hold the rope, not to let it out any more. Then, gripping the rope over her head, she pumped her legs as if she were on a swing and started a long pendulum-like motion.

Under us, toward the steel.

Out, over the rock, till the rope stretched taut.

In again, farther in, out of sight. Into the steel.

Then out, out toward the treetops.

The rope burned between my palms.

She swung out . . . then in . . . then out again . . . then in . . .

"More rope," she called. Jeff came forward against the sill. He was sweating. "What's she doing? Where is she?"

"I can't see her now," I said. "She's underneath."

The rope snapped against Jeff's body.

"Rope! Give me rope . . ." Her voice seemed thin, fading.

I untied the rope from Jeff's waist. Jeff and I held the end together, playing it out as far as it would go. "That's all," I called down. The rope snapped against our hands, then suddenly went slack. I tugged, and it came up loose. "Wendy!" I yelled.

Ed came flying over. "You creeps, what'd you do?"

He punched me, then grabbed the rope. It came up slack and empty in his hands. A look of horror was on his face.

From below us there was a shout. A cry of triumph. "I'm free!" Wendy was on the stairs. We all rushed to the trapdoor. "Free!"

"Wendy," Jeff yelled, pounding on the door with his fists, "I could kiss you!"

"Wendy!" Ed cried. "Wendy, Wendy, Wendy."

We were all laughing and yelling back and forth. Then Wendy started the tedious work of prying the knotted chains apart. We three tried forcing the trapdoor, but it only made the knots tighter. There was nothing to do but wait.

It was a wonderful moment when Wendy called, "All clear," and the trapdoor came up. We shook hands ceremoniously all around. Then we started down. I helped Ed, who almost cried with relief when his feet touched solid ground. Wendy came after with Jeff.

We ran to the path. "Hurry," I said. "Let's get away from here!"

15

The light was nearly gone. The woods were damp, shadowy. My first happy rush of hope at being free had disappeared. We splashed across the stream. Jeff stumbled and almost lost his footing. I caught his arm.

"Go on, go ahead," he said. "Don't wait for me." He pushed me forward. "Just get out of here as fast as you can."

Behind him Wendy was coming down the path barefoot. She helped Jeff while I rushed down the path after Ed. His height sickness had disappeared as soon as he touched solid ground, and now he was nearly out of sight.

"Wait up," I called as he disappeared around a turn in the path. It was getting darker every minute, and I was afraid we'd get separated. I ducked under a branch, caught a glimpse of a boot. I barely had time to realize that it was too big to be Ed's when Bogie grabbed me.

I struggled in his grip. "Run!" I yelled at the top of my lungs. "Wendy! Jeff! *Run!*"

Bogie knocked me to the ground. Pearl appeared, dragging Ed by the hair. She pushed him down next to me.

Bogie crashed through the woods. *Wendy . . . get away . . . run . . . don't let him hear you . . .* They couldn't go far with Jeff nearly blind. *Hide, Jeff . . . get down somewhere . . . under a bush . . . don't breathe . . .*

"Why'd you come back?" I said despairingly.

"Ask your father," she said. "He must be stupid! He can't even follow simple directions, show up where he's supposed to. I thought you had to be smart to be rich."

"Didn't he come?" I said.

"He came all right. Waited in the hotel just like I told him. Said he had the money. He led us a merry chase from phone booth to phone booth all day. But when it came to nuts and bolts, when payday came, he never showed up! No Chapman! No money! What do you think of that? Think your father wants his money more than he wants you?"

"Something must have happened," I said. I couldn't think what. My mind blurred. We'd tried so hard to get away . . . we'd come so close . . .

"Something happened all right!" Pearl exploded. "Your father started counting his money. He put you on the scale, and you lost. Listen! Bogie can't handle this grief. He gets all excited, he gets upset. Things go wrong, he goes crazy." She pointed the gun at me.

"Just remember, anything bad happens, it's your fault."

"Something bad has happened already," I burst out. "You shot Pam!"

"Shut up about that! Whose idea was it for her to run away? Yours?" She cracked me across the face. "Your father gets one more chance to get his little boy back, and that's it. Bogie," she yelled, "get back here."

We heard him crashing around in the dark.

Wendy . . . Jeff . . . Where were they? If only I hadn't argued with Wendy about going out on the rope, had said yes the moment she suggested it. If only we'd done everything faster, sooner, better. If only . . . if only . . .

Crack . . .

I groaned. Ed's face crumpled.

Crack . . . *crack*

Bogie ran up, waving the gun. "I got them. I got them! Let's go." They yanked us up and pushed us like two robots down the path. Numbness overcame me—the numbness of too much horror. Ed fell against me. I caught him. We staggered on.

The van was just off the road, deep in the shadow of a hill. They pushed us in and locked the door. As they did, something struck the side of the van. I thought it was a gunshot. I hardly reacted. I just lay there. There were two more terrific cracks into the van.

"They're stones," Ed said. "Somebody's shooting stones."

It took a moment for me to make the connection, to realize it could only be Jeff or Wendy. *Bogie hadn't hit them.*

More rocks pelted the van. Glass shattered. They were breaking the windows.

Bogie started screaming. Then they were shooting. *Crack . . . crack . . . crack crack crack . . .* It sounded as if a war had broken out. The noise was deafening.

Ed and I pounded on the side of the van. "Get away! Run. Wendy, Jeff, don't let him . . . run, run . . . *go!*"

The rock throwing stopped. Then the shooting stopped.

"We got them!" Bogie's voice shook with excitement. "We got them this time."

"Come on. We've got to get out of here."

Doors slammed. The engine turned over. The van lurched forward. "I saw that darky jump out from behind a tree," Bogie said. "He isn't going to talk to anyone any more. And neither will that ugly little redhead."

Ed threw himself against the partition. "You filthy murderers! You dirty killers, I'll get you."

"Shut up," Pearl screamed. "You're next, just remember that."

I pulled Ed down, held him down the best I could.

He tried to knock me away, but I held him, just held him till he wasn't fighting any more. I crouched next to him, my eyes clenched shut, feeling a despair, an emptiness I'd never known before. We'd been five, and there had been hope and life, and something to look forward to. Now we were two, and I couldn't understand why all these things had happened. I couldn't understand the reason any more for the whole hideous drama of the kidnapping.

I only wanted it to end. I wanted to wake up and discover it had all been a terrible dream. *Bring the curtain down*, I pleaded. *This play stinks*. Nobody listened.

Ed's sobs subsided.

The van lurched from side to side. "Slow down!" Pearl said. "We don't want the cops on us. Bad enough we have that broken headlight."

"We've got to get rid of this stupid van," Bogie said. "Drive into the city, dump this heap. You get the car, call Chapman again. Jesus, I'm sick of calling him! That stupid bastard—if he went to the cops—"

"No way," Pearl said. "If he were with the cops he would have been Johnny-on-the-spot with the money. Stay calm! We just have to stay cool and stay with it."

Hadn't I lived through all this once before? I shut my ears to their babble. I didn't want to listen. How many times would I have to go through it before it all ended?

Ed and I said little. Everything we'd tried had turned out horribly. Burning down the boathouse. Pam's trying to escape. Wendy's risking her life on the rope. Her and Jeff's running. What for? What good had any of it done? When the van stopped, neither of us moved. We heard her get out. "You can get a bus here," he said. "Get the car. I'll do my bit."

He pulled back onto the road again. Once I glanced listlessly through the bolt hole. I saw street lights, empty unfamiliar streets, then a dark road. The van stopped. Bogie got out. A gate creaked. Then he was back, the van moving slowly down a bumpy road. Rocks struck the underside. He stopped again. I heard the shrill cry of peepers. I smelled swampy water. Bogie opened the back door. He flashed the light in Ed's face. "You. Over here."

Ed backed away. Bogie reached in, pulled Ed down to his knees, yanked his hands behind him, and tied him up. He stuffed a gag in Ed's mouth.

He ordered me to sit away from Ed. He left the back door open, then sat down on a rock where he could watch me and lit a cigarette. We were in the middle of an empty car-wrecking yard. I could see dark, splintered trees and the shadowy hulks of cars. Far away I heard the sounds of the highway.

Bogie finished one cigarette and lit another. He got up and paced around, then sat down again. He must have smoked half a pack of cigarettes. Ed lay helpless on the floor.

Help him, Derek.

What for? It will only make things worse. Everything has made things worse.

Help him, Derek.

I watched Bogie. When he turned away for an instant, I inched closer to Ed. I got close enough to touch him, then to start working on his gag. Bogie swung around. I jumped back.

"What are you doing? Get over here!" He dragged me out of the van and locked Ed in. Worse, always worse.

A car was coming. He pulled me around the side of the van and locked his arm around my throat. The car was closer, coming toward us.

A horn beeped lightly three times, then once again. A signal. He pushed me forward, up a hill. A darkened car was waiting. He whistled, and Pearl got out.

"How'd it go?" he said.

"Couldn't be better."

"You have any trouble getting the car?"

"No, why should I? Just paid the lot fee and drove off."

"What about Chapman?" he asked.

"Mis-ter Chapman," she said, "is waiting on us once more. Resigned, penitent, and eager to serve."

"All right, Pearl, don't talk like that. What happened to him? Why the hell didn't he show up with the money? What's his excuse this time?"

She took his cigarette and drew on it. "Simple. He got caught in a traffic jam. The fool drove straight into the G.E. traffic on Erie Boulevard and got tied up for an hour."

Bogie swore. "You believe that?"

"I told you, if he went to the cops they'd make sure he got where he was supposed to. What do you say we get going."

She opened the trunk of the car. "In you go, Derek."

My heart jerked convulsively. I struggled in Bogie's grip. "Hold him," she said. They tied me hand and foot, and gagged me with an oily rag. Then the two of them pushed me into the trunk and slammed the lid down.

16

I lost track of time, the number of times they stopped.

Fumes filled the trunk. I was dizzy, nauseated. My eyes closed. The motor throbbed. I saw faces . . . rushing figures . . . animals . . . I was with Mom and Ora . . . going to the opera. I was all dressed up. A little kid. My mother's gown . . . velvet, deep blue velvet that slipped through my fingers like water. My mother laughing, "Derek's falling asleep."

Someone knocked, three sharp knocks. I heard a voice. "They're going to kill you, Derek."

I woke with a start. *You don't dare sleep.* The voice was in my head. Not my voice. Clear. Calm. Neither male nor female. *They killed Pam, Jeff, Wendy. You didn't see the bodies, but that's what they did. Shot to kill. Left Ed to die in the van. You're next. Sleep and the fumes will get you. You'll be as dead as the others. Are you listening? What're they saying now? Listen!*

"I told him I was watching him," Pearl was saying. "You should have seen his head jerk around."

"Why'd you say that? He didn't see you, did he?"

"How could he? I was in the restaurant and he was outside, across the street in the phone booth at the gas station. I just watched him through the window. He couldn't see me."

"You were taking a crazy chance."

"I liked it. I have to get something out of this. I wanted to go right out and knock on the phone booth. Just to see his face up close. His big-shot face. 'Here I am, Mr. Chapman, your son's kidnapper. What are you going to do about it?' "

Were my eyes open? *Open your eyes! Think. What are you going to do?*

I worked math problems. When I blurred on that I named the states in alphabetical order. Then I listed all the bluegrass songs and composers I knew. I hummed the songs.

That the best you can do? What a voice. Sing like that and they'll shoot you sure.

I'm trying. Doing the best I can.

Work on those ropes. Fight.

I'm trying. They have me tied up like a chicken in a bag.

Stay awake, be alert. Don't sleep. Never sleep.

I'm not. I'm not.

I worked my arms and legs, tensed my muscles against the ropes, relaxed, tensed again.

Exercise, that's it, keep the old arms and legs loose. If they untie you, run . . . run for your life . . .

Okay. Run for my life. *Fuga salutem peter,* run for one's life . . . *amo, amas, amat,* I love, you love, he loves, *amare ce,* I love myself . . . I love Pam, does she love me, Pam is dead, dead, run for your life, Derek, *fuga salutem peter,* Mr. Kapzio would be proud of me now, Latin is a comfort, he tells the first-year students . . . ha, ha, good for a laugh every time . . . Kapzio with his big puff of hair, must comb it ten times a day, spitting and salivating every time he reads to us from Caesar . . . Nobody really understands, nobody listens. Not true. Danforth. Top student . . . Frank Danforth, big football hero, likes Latin too . . .

Latin is a comfort . . . *veni, vidi, vici* . . . Wenus wowed wengence on Wincent Wiceroy. When I get back to school I'll get to that Latin in earnest . . . earnestly . . . sincerely.

I woke with my heart churning, an awful taste in my mouth, my head clotted with fumes.

Pearl was talking. "You ready to send him to delivery? It's time."

My heart jumped to my throat. Delivery . . . deliver me from evil . . . *you're dead, Derek.* No! I'm not dead yet. No. No.

When they stopped again I knew we were on a bridge. I heard the steady thump-thump-thump of passing traffic and below the high-pitched whine of a highway.

"You told him what to do, where to—"

"Yes. How many times— Give me the binoculars."

There was a long, suffocating silence.

"Oh, my god, that's him," she exclaimed. "The white car. He's taking out the garbage bags."

"Let me see."

"Wait. Okay. They're in the can. *The bags are in the can.* Let's go."

"Anybody around? You see anybody? Make sure—"

"Clear. Clear! He's gone. Come on, no more waiting."

The car moved off. Rumbled across the bridge. Turned onto the highway. Stopped. One of them got out. A thud over my head. Another thud. Then Pearl: "Okay. Go. Nice and easy. Take the next exit." Her voice was thin, tightly controlled.

I was fully alert now, tense, trying to think, to plan. They had the money. *They no longer need you, Derek.*

"Is it all there?" he said. "Count it."

"Count it? Are you kidding! It'll take days to count it!"

"I don't trust him. Open it up. Count it!"

I heard her moving around. Then: "It's here all right. Look at this! It's unbelievable. Our money. Our beautiful, beautiful money. All the money we'll ever want. Here, honey, smell it! Kiss it!" The car swerved. They were both laughing. "Did you ever see such beautiful garbage?"

"Cut it out," he said. "That's enough, put it away, you're making me nervous. Anybody sees us—"

"Anybody sees us out here on this back road, they're going to think we're out to dump our trash like all the rest of the slobs. Or maybe you think the cows are watching?"

"Very funny," he said.

"You betcha it's funny. God, I could laugh! Laugh till I bust! Bogie, we did it. Bogie, Bogie—hey, sourpuss, we did it!"

"Better stop with that 'Bogie' business now," he said after a while.

"Right. Funny how I almost got so I believed it. Bogie and Pearl. You Bogie. Me Pearl."

"You were right about that, anyway. Having us practice using the names before—"

"Sure I was right. I'm right about lots of things."

"You've got brains."

"You're all right yourself. You know that? You're terrific, you're great, and now you're rich." She burst out laughing.

"Where we going to dump him? Let's get it over with."

"We could take him with us, just take him for a nice long ride across the country—"

"Don't say stuff like that. You make me nervous. I want to get rid of him. After that, we're clean. And you better think where we're getting rid of the guns when we're through."

"Told you that already. That bridge over the Mohawk—keep driving, I'm looking for a good spot."

Sweat burst out all over me. *Stay calm, Derek. Think. They want to kill you, but you want to live. You're going to live, you're going to live, you're going*

*to live, you hear me, you're going to fight. Fight. Not
dead till proved dead. Think. What are you going
to do?*

That voice again. Neutral. Fearless. Mine? I heard
it, listened to it, agreed with it.

But I wasn't fearless and calm. I swallowed back a
spurt of nausea. All they had to do was open the
trunk, put the gun to my head, fire.

"Here?" he asked.

"Not yet."

"Let's get rid of him!"

"I'm looking, don't get excited—"

"Don't start on me," he said. "What about here?"

"No. That farmhouse. Keep going, keep going."

"You don't have to tell me everything twice."

"Watch it, the ditch. The ditch!"

"Knock it off!" He slammed on the brakes. "This
is it."

Footsteps.

The trunk was raised.

Cold air rushed into my lungs. My eyes streamed
water.

He grabbed me under the arms. She took my legs.
They hauled me out of the car. I saw the back end of
it, a black car, the license plate . . .

"Up that hill," she said. "Out of sight."

They carried me across a ditch and up a wooded
hill, dragging me between them. *Wait! The plan was
you'd untie me and then I'd run for it.*

They were panting. "Enough," she said. "This is far enough."

They dropped me. Birds were singing. The fields smelled of manure. I looked up at them. She was wearing the belted trench coat, the red scarf. He had on a fringed jacket. His face was puffy. They didn't look evil, only ordinary.

My heart jerked behind my ribs. He bent over, pushing me, rolling me deeper into the underbrush like a bundle of rags. I saw his face over me. Those narrow squeezed-up eyes. Sweat poured off his face. He raised his gun.

I threw myself over, rolled over and over, rolled for my life.

"Hey," she said, "look at him." She was laughing, a nervous, high-pitched laugh. "Just like a worm. Get it over with, will you."

Click . . . My body tensed against the impact. Mom. Good-bye. I'm sorry . . .

Click . . . *click* . . .

I was still rolling. Still alive.

"What's wrong with this freakin' gun?" he shouted.

"*Is it loaded?*" she asked, emphasizing each word. "I bet you forgot to reload it."

"Goddammit, where's your gun?"

"In the car."

"In the car! What's it doing there?" he shouted. "Go get it."

I rolled over the ground. Roll, roll, roll, roll, but as

much as I rolled, I could still see them. They could still see me. Three strides and he'd have me.

"Well, go on," he said.

"Wait—" She grabbed his arm. "Listen!"

The sound of a slowly throbbing engine filled the air.

"Somebody's down there on the road," she said. "They're going to see the car. Wait! They're on the *hill*. They're coming up the hill!"

"A tractor," he said. "It's a tractor. Some freakin' chickenshit farmer on his tractor."

The engine grew louder and closer.

"It's coming this way," she said. "It's coming up the hill."

They both froze, listening.

"It's coming," she said. "Let's get out of here."

"What about him?" He ran toward me and clubbed me with his gun, hitting me on the head and neck.

"Come on!" she exclaimed. "Push him out of sight."

He kicked me again, pushed me under some bushes, and threw some branches over me. Then they both ran.

I lay there, dazed from the blows, tasting blood in my mouth.

I heard them running down the hill. Then I heard the car roar to life. They drove away. The sound of the tractor grew fainter also, then receded completely. I was alone. Alone and alive.

I felt a single rush of pure joy. The smell of the

earth, the sound of the early morning breeze, the light spreading through the trees—the world had never seemed so perfect.

They were gone! My heart was pounding like mad. *Gone.*

Slowly I calmed down.

I was still tied, bound and gagged.

I brought my knees up to my chest and pushed like an inchworm. Bit by bit I inched myself to the crest of the hill. Below, the empty road curved out of sight.

What if they were parked just around that curve, waiting? Still waiting to kill me? *Hide! Hide under a bush. Hide anywhere.*

My skin shriveled. I felt a deep, instinctive need to bury myself deep in shadows, in a cave, under a rock. To be safe. To nurse my hurt body.

They could be creeping up the other side of the hill right now. Creeping toward me. My limbs jerked. My back felt raw, exposed. I twisted myself around. Something scurried in the leaves. A black bird flew by, crying shrilly. Calling a warning. *The killers are coming back . . . coming back . . . coming back for you.* I wanted to run, run, run, never stop till I had run so far they couldn't find me.

I thrashed frantically, imprisoned in the ropes. I went off balance and slid over the crest of the hill into more stones and scrubby bushes. I pitched and slid down the hill, over stones and through trees. Now that

I was moving, I couldn't go fast enough. I squirmed, twisted, threw myself down the hill, and fell straight into a ditch on the side of the road.

Like a dog, I pushed my face into the soggy, leaf-filled water. I was parched. Water soaked through the gag. The cuts in my face throbbed.

Listen. They're coming back to kill you. Listen. I raised my head. For a moment all I could hear was the sound of my own heart. Then a cow bellowed in the distance. A dog barked.

Listen.

Remember. You're a witness.

They want you dead. Be careful. You can live.

Through the earth I felt the sound of rushing feet. I slid back into the water and pressed myself frantically into the mud and leaves. The pounding feet came closer. Shaking the earth. Pounding toward me. Then a girl with her hair loose galloped past me on a horse. It was like a dream.

I pushed myself up the muddy bank, shouting, my voice lost in the gag.

The girl looked around. She looked up into the air, as if she thought she'd heard a bird screaming. I shouted ferociously, wordlessly. *Here I am. Here! Here!*

My head was level with the road. She saw me.

"Hey! Who are you?" She dismounted and threw the reins over the horse's head. Slowly she walked back toward me. She was wearing jeans and rubber boots.

I tried to get up on the road. *Hurry up. Hurry. Hurry! The killers are coming back.*

About five feet from me, she stopped. She wiped her hands down the sides of her jeans. "What is this, a fraternity stunt?" She kept looking at me as if she couldn't decide if she should untie me or just leave me there.

I screamed again.

She stepped backward.

I inched myself up on the road. I lay still. I didn't scream again.

Finally, she approached me, knelt down, and untied the gag from behind my head. "Okay, what's it all about?"

"Kidnapped," I cried hoarsely. "Untie me, for god's sake. Hurry!" But the words came out a gabble. I could barely move my jaws.

She looked at me fearfully.

"Untie me, damn it! Untie me!"

"Whew. Take it easy. You bite, too?" Gingerly she started working on the knots.

"Faster! Don't you have a knife with you? They might be coming back."

"Who?"

"The kidnappers." My hands were free. I bent over and picked at the knots around my ankles. My fingers were clumsy, almost useless.

"Are you serious about this kidnapper stuff?"

"Yes! Get this knot out. Come on, work at it!" I threw off the last rope and stood up. I was wobbly and had to sit down again. *But just for a minute. Get up!* "I need a phone. Where do you live? I've got to phone the police."

"We're down the road about two miles. No phone, though." She swung up on her horse. "Sit here. I'll go back and get the jeep. You don't look so good." She mounted her horse and galloped down the road, raising a cloud of dust behind her.

"Wait!" I yelled. But she didn't hear me. I followed, taking a few steps, then stopped to listen. The road was still. I could hear the tractor again in the distance. I walked along the shoulder, one eye searching out hiding places.

Around the turn I heard a car.

I dove into the bushes.

The car stopped. Someone got out.

Get up, Derek. Run.

"Hey, it's me," a girl's voice called behind me. "Where you going? It's me, Lydia. I brought you an orange."

17

"You must be starved," Lydia said. We were sitting in her jeep. I licked my lips. I'd eaten the orange, peel and all. I had forgotten how good food was.

She looked at me curiously. "I should have brought you another orange. Come back to the farmhouse, I'll really feed you. We're a commune. We always have visitors. Buckwheat pancakes and fresh cow's butter for breakfast. Don't those cuts hurt? I brought some stuff to put on them."

She had a little kit with tape and antiseptic and fixed up the cut on my head. "Hold still, I've had a lot of experience since I went on the farm. I'm good at this. I bet you won't even need stitches."

"I want a phone," I said.

"I'm sorry, we don't have one at the farm. The closest phone is out on the highway, at the Four Corners."

"Let's go then." She still didn't start the jeep.

"I have to grain the animals, and it's my week to

milk Heidi. As soon as I get that stuff done, I'll drive you—Hey! Where're you going?"

I'd climbed out of the jeep. I couldn't sit there and chitchat.

"Wait a minute." Lydia coasted up in the jeep. "What's the matter with you? You aren't going to find a phone very fast that way. Come on, get in."

"Will you drive me to the phone?"

She looked annoyed. "Oh, okay. But I'm going to get it from the others when I get back. You know, you can't overlook a cow that needs milking. It's not a light matter."

I looked both ways, up and down the road.

"It's too bad we don't have a phone at the farm, but we voted against it. It's more natural. Say, Derek," she said a moment later, "where do you live when you're not being kidnapped?"

She was smiling. She was talking as if we were just driving along a country road on a fresh early morning, having a nice time, a nice drive, a nice conversation. I couldn't reply. I couldn't connect to the words. I couldn't have a conversation, just *talk*.

For days I'd thought of nothing but the kidnapping. I couldn't shake it off. I still wasn't really free of them. At every turn I tensed, expecting to see their car.

"You don't talk much, do you?" she said.

I twisted around, thinking that Bogie had doubled back and they were behind us.

"Hey, can't you relax?" she said, glancing at my hands. "You look ready to jump out of your skin."

"Where'd you say that phone was?"

"Not far." She pushed her hair back.

We came to the end of the dirt road. I stared at the long open stretch of highway ahead. "How far now?"

"About five more miles. You know, there was nothing in the paper about you being kidnapped."

"I've been kidnapped!" I shouted, going into a rage. How could she be so thick? I held up my wrists, showing her the welts. I pointed to my head. "You think I did this to myself? Hurry up!"

I sank back against the seat. I was making myself sick. I had to save my strength. Was that me flying into a rage, ordering people around?

The Four Corners turned out to be two gas pumps and one square wooden building closed up tight. The phone was inside. "You can wait here," Lydia said. "They'll be opening up soon."

"Where's another phone booth?"

"Fifteen miles. Your best bet is wait right here."

"I'm not waiting! You've got to drive me."

"I told you, I have to get back to the farm." She pressed her lips together. "And you don't have to shout at me. I didn't have to help you!"

The burst of rage passed.

"Lydia, I'm sorry. It's the others—" I was unable to control my voice. "I'm sorry. Please, will you take me? I need your help."

She tapped her fingers against the steering wheel and threw me a sidelong glance. Then she nodded. "But don't you shout at me again."

"I won't."

I sat back, looking at the road ahead. The country-side passed like a film, patches of woods . . . the fog just burning off the fields . . . fences . . . hedgerows . . . cows grazing. It was so peaceful. So false.

Ahead I saw the long white stretch of the Interstate Bridge. Cars were pulled over on the shoulder of the road. A gray state-police car with a flashing red light blocked the highway. Troopers in gray uniforms were stopping every vehicle.

Lydia groaned. "A license check, I bet. And I left mine home!" She started to make a U-turn.

"Don't!" I said. A tall, uniformed trooper blew a piercing blast on his whistle. He walked rapidly to-ward us, holding up his arms. "Hold it!" he yelled.

I got out and hobbled toward him.

"Get back in that jeep," he called. "You're supposed to stay in line. No U-turns."

"Sir, I have to talk to you—"

"Wait your turn." He had me by the arm, rushing me back to the jeep.

"Wait, listen. I'm Derek Chapman. I was kid-napped, and I need the police."

He stopped, held me at arm's length. "What hap-pened to your face? You have any identification?"

Lydia leaned out of the jeep. "He's telling you the truth, Officer. I found him tied up on Mud Mill Road. I untied him myself. We've been looking for a phone—"

I spoke urgently over her voice. "It's not just me,

they kidnapped four other kids, too. Shot them, shot—"

"*Four* others?" His voice tightened. Did he think I was lying? He turned to Lydia. "Let me see your license." He bent down to inspect her tires.

"I've got nothing to do with this." She started to explain again about finding me in the ditch.

Another trooper was walking toward us. I turned toward him. Maybe he'd listen to me. "Hold on there," the first trooper snapped, his hand on his holster. It was crazy.

"Listen," I began, "I'm telling you the truth. I'm Derek Chap—" I broke off. Ahead, almost at the head of the line of cars parked on the shoulder, I saw a familiar bulky figure getting out of a black car. "It's him! It's him!" I rushed forward. "It's Bogie!"

18

"Bogie!"

Half out of his car, he turned, saw me, stared as if he didn't recognize me. He'd never expected to see me again, and certainly not here.

"It's me!" I yelled. He thought he could knock me around, tie me up, shoot me, throw me away like trash and forget me. But here I was! I wasn't so easy to get rid of! I felt an enormous satisfaction, a singing sensation in my skin. Fatigue rolled off me. Air rushed into my lungs. Bogie seemed to be waiting for me. I leaped forward, an inarticulate cry of triumph filling my throat. I had forgotten fear. I was yelling, pointing to him, "Get him!" And still he stood there.

Then, suddenly, he ducked back into his car. I ran forward. "Don't let him go! Stop him!" The car jerked out of line. It sped around the roadblock. Chaos followed: shouts, whistles, gunfire. People ducked for cover.

Near me a patrol car swung out in pursuit. As it

passed, I opened the door and jumped into the back seat. The trooper in the passenger seat whirled on me. "Who the hell—"

"I'm Derek Chapman. That's them—the ones who kidnapped me—in the black car. Don't let them get away!" I leaned over the front seat between the two troopers, telling them about the kidnapping. It poured out of me. "There were five of us—" I told them everything. I was afraid they wouldn't believe me, so I started to tell them again.

The dark trooper with a mustache took notes, writing down the names of the others. He told me the roadblock had been set up to find me, after my father went to the police. The driver radioed into headquarters. A scratchy voice answered his report. "We do have a missing persons on those four names. All four. Four kids disappeared last Saturday. We've got an eighty-six on everyone. Who'd you say you got there?"

"The Chapman kid. Derek Chapman."

"Where'd he come from?"

"Popped into the car like a rabbit."

The car roared forward, its siren clearing the way. I kept my eyes fixed on the road ahead. Bogie's car had disappeared.

"Chapman is here at seventy," the voice on the intercom reported. "He's anxious about his son. You sure you got him okay?"

"It's me," I said, leaning over the front seat. "Tell my father I'm okay. I'm okay now." I couldn't stop talking. "They shot Pam and left her," I told the trooper with the mustache again. "Left her in the woods. That was—" I hesitated. "What day is it now?"

"Thursday."

"Thursday! They kidnapped us Saturday. They shot Pam—it was yesterday morning. Yesterday morning? Wednesday? I can't get the time straight."

"Calm down, kid," the driver said, without turning around. "You're safe now, it's all over."

All over? No it wasn't. It would never be all over. Not even if they caught Bogie and Pearl and sent them to jail for life.

Pam . . . get up, Pam . . . don't just lie there . . . get up and run . . .

"Hey, you okay?" The trooper turned around. "Take it easy."

I looked past him. Bogie's car had disappeared. "Can't you go any faster? Go faster! Is this the fastest you can go?"

The driver snorted. "Listen to the speedo. We're going over a hundred now. We'll get them."

The intercom crackled. Roadblocks were being set up at all intersections. A helicopter was being dispatched.

The countryside passed in a blur. Here and there, little white houses sat back from the road. Cars . . . bikes . . . a line of washing . . . People were going about their normal lives while we roared down the highway, siren screaming.

The intercom jittered again. "You want to put the Chapman boy on the mike? His father's anxious to talk to him."

The driver leaned forward. "Forget it. We've got them in sight again."

I looked through the windshield. Ahead, far ahead, I caught a glint of metal. My heart leaped. I pressed against the seat willing the car to move faster. The speedometer needle moved steadily upward: 102 . . . 104 . . . 105 . . . *We're going to catch you now, Bogie . . . Are you scared? . . . Are you looking over your shoulder, Pearl? . . . I'm coming for you now . . . You're going to be caught . . . caught, caught, like a fish in a net . . .*

The siren wailed. Cars slid aside. I could see the black car now, swerving from lane to lane. We were closing the gap. I saw the license plate. I saw Bogie bent over the wheel. We were gaining on them.

Suddenly he braked and swerved sharply right, then left, throwing up a cloud of smoke and gravel. The car skidded and rattled across the grassy meridian dividing the highway, straight across the road toward a cluster of yellow construction machines. Then it disappeared.

I groaned out loud.

"Hold on!" The driver wrenched his wheel around. Tires screamed. We skidded over the unpaved shoulder, spitting gravel. The black car reappeared, on the road again, going in the wrong direction.

We pursued them, racing directly toward oncoming traffic. Horns blared. Cars flew off the road. I hung on to the back of the seat. We were overtaking them. I could see both of them plainly. Pearl was bent over toward the back. "They've got guns," I said.

"Get down." The trooper leaned out and fired his revolver. Once, twice. The black car veered from side to side.

We pursued them past an airport exit, past a diner, a cluster of homes, and up a long curving overpass. Below us was a vast shopping center with a parking lot; people small as ants looked up curiously. The siren screamed. Bogie's car wobbled from lane to lane. There was a turnoff to the right, a feeder from the highway. Bogie swung right, down the turnoff. A car was coming up the incline, directly toward them.

The black car swerved, hit a guardrail, then spun across the pavement, slammed into another guardrail, and, almost in slow motion, rose over the edge of the railing. The doors opened; the car hovered in the air, then dropped out of sight.

The trooper slammed on the brakes and wrenched open the door. "Stay here," he ordered. Both troopers ran. I ran after them.

Below me, in the parking lot, the car lay on its back, the wheels still spinning. A cloud of dust drifted away. An arm was thrust through the windshield. Black liquid ran out on the pavement.

I hung on the crumpled guardrail, my legs trembling. Money spilled out of the car. The wind picked up the bills and swirled them around. People ran toward the car and scrambled for the money. Then I saw Bogie, crawling, one leg dragging, trying to shut the door on the money.

19

A crowd of reporters and TV people with big black cameras perched on their shoulders was hovering outside the Public Safety Building. As the troopers' car pulled into a parking space, I caught sight of my father. "Dad!" I cried, rolling down the window.

Tie askew, jacket open, shorter and rougher-looking than every other person in that crowd, my father stood out unmistakably like a thornbush in a garden. I opened the car door and half stepped out. "Dad." He didn't hear me. He was being bombarded with questions.

"Mr. Chapman," a reporter called, "did you ever despair of your son's life?"

"Would you, if it were your son?" he asked her.

"Mr. Chapman, Mr. Chapman, sir, is it true that you turned over more than a million dollars to the kidnappers?"

"Half a million."

"Sir, did you have any trouble raising that much cash?"

"No. Why should I?"

"Do you expect to recover all that money, Mr. Chapman?"

"I hope to."

"Dad!" I started walking toward him. He saw me then, over the heads of the reporters. "Hello, Dad," I called. I was grinning ... choking ...

"Derek!" he cried. At the sound of my name the entire crowd of reporters turned, forcing their mikes and cameras into my face, coming like a wall between me and Dad.

"It's Derek."

"It's the kidnapped boy."

"Derek, how do you feel now that your ordeal is over?"

Flashbulbs popped. Their voices surrounded me.

"Is it true that you were kidnapped along with four other young people, but that you alone survive?"

"Would you say something about the conditions which you experienced during your captivity, Derek?"

"Did they treat you well? What are your feelings about the kidnappers now that they've been caught?"

I threw up my hands against the onslaught. It was like an attack. I didn't know which way to turn.

"Leave him alone!" Dad pushed people aside left and right and strode toward me. "Derek. Derek—" He held out his arms.

I felt lightheaded, overcome with emotion. For a single instant I saw Dad clearly—the way other people must see him, the way I'd never really seen him before: a short, muscular man, something fierce radiating from him. Power. Energy. A force that allowed him to push through a crowd and make people stand aside—and not mind. Feel they *should* stand aside. He was Jimmy Neal Chapman. The kidnapping had happened because I was his son, but *it had happened to me.* Something awful and terribly important that belonged to Derek Chapman alone.

Then Dad grabbed me in his arms and hugged me, and all I felt was a wrenching gladness to be with him again, in his arms, safe and protected.

The flashbulbs popped in our eyes. "Mr. Chapman, how does it feel to have your son back?"

"Let's get out of here." Dad pushed me into the troopers' car and got in beside me, slamming and locking the doors. "Get us away from here," he said to the driver, who was writing something down on a clipboard.

"Sir?" The trooper looked around.

"I'm Chapman. Get us away from these newspaper vultures."

The trooper drove us away.

"Derek, let me look at you." He gripped me by the arms. "God, I'm glad to see you." His eyes darkened. He touched my forehead where Lydia had taped it, then my cheek. "What did they do to you? You're a mass of bruises."

I shook my head. I didn't dare speak. I was afraid the floodgates would open and I'd bawl like a little kid.

"We're going to be followed, Mr. Chapman," the trooper said. "No way to stop it. You're news now, you and your son."

"Just drive around for a while," Dad said. "My son and I have to talk. I'll clear it with your superiors."

Quickly I told Dad the things that had happened. How we were tied and gagged. The fire. When they shot Pam.

"Derek, I never want to live through six days like this again." Dad's voice trembled. "The worst time for me was last night after I dropped the money in that godforsaken rest area. And you weren't there. All the time they'd been promising me—give us the money and we'll give you back your son. I thought the worst." He looked around. We were being followed by the reporters and TV people. "You better drive us to the Washington Inn," he told the trooper.

"I've taken a suite there," he said to me. "You need a shower, medical attention, food, rest—" His voice filled. "Derek, I'll make this up to you."

"There's nothing to make up, Dad." I felt again as I had when I first saw him. He and I were connected, but not one. I was a separate person.

The driver stopped for a red light. I leaned forward. "I want to go back to the Public Safety Building."

"Derek," Dad said, "those reporters will eat you up alive. I'm getting you away from—"

"Dad, didn't they tell you? There were four other kids. I have to go back. If you want to go to the hotel, it's okay. I'll meet you there later." I started to open the car door.

My father caught my hand. "Let's talk about this—"

The waves of power and persuasion were rolling over me now, as they had all my life. *Let's talk about this . . . I think it would be best if you . . . I've given this a lot of thought, and it seems apparent to me . . .*

I freed my hand. "Dad, I'm going back." We just looked at each other for a moment. Then I spoke to the trooper. "Who should I see at the Public Safety Building?"

"Lieutenant Gordon. I'll drive you there." The trooper swung the car around.

Dad spoke first. "You've changed," he said. "You've changed, haven't you, Derek?" He knotted up his tie, then almost at once pulled it loose again. "You're right, of course." Then, as if he'd made a decision, he tapped my knee. "Good," he said. "Very good."

At the PSB, my father said he'd distract the reporters to give me time to get to Lieutenant Gordon's office. "I'll wait for you."

Inside I was directed to the second-floor office, an open glass-walled room, then to Lieutenant Gordon's cubicle. "Come on in, Derek. I'm glad you're here." He shut the door. There was a coffee container and a glazed doughnut on his desk. "Can I get you something? A cup of coffee?" I shook my head. "How about milk and a doughnut? These doughnuts are fresh."

"Nothing. Thank you." I wasn't hungry. It was strange. I had hardly eaten for days, but I had almost no interest in food. "Water is all I want." I started to get up, but he motioned me back.

"Let me," he said. He drew a paper cup of water from a glass dispenser in the corner and handed it to me. I drained it in one gulp. Lieutenant Gordon sat down behind his desk. He was a big, freckled man. There was a picture of two smiling freckled girls hanging behind the desk.

"Well, Derek, where do we start?"

I leaned forward. "Have you found out anything about the other kids? Have you talked to Bogie and Pearl?"

"Your kidnappers? Not much chance of that, unfortunately. The woman isn't expected to live. She's bleeding internally. The last report on the man, he was on the operating table, in serious condition. The important thing now is to find the other four people taken with you. Suppose you tell me briefly what happened, and then we'll go back over the details."

I related the whole story from beginning to end. Lieutenant Gordon took notes on a yellow pad. When I finished he got me another glass of water and patted my shoulder.

"All right. Now—" He held up a sheet of paper. "Pamela Barbushek. Edward Hill. Jefferson Wyatt. Wendy Manheim." He read off their names. "Let's go over what happened to each of them."

I tried to speak dryly. "Pam was shot. They killed her and left her. They shot Wendy and Jeff. I think they're dead too. Ed's locked in the van, tied and gagged. They left him to die. They tried to kill me, too, after they got the money, but Bogie had forgotten to reload his gun."

Lieutenant Gordon ran his hands over his freckled face. He looked really upset. He stood and called to another policeman to check on the kidnappers at the hospital. "Let me know the minute we can talk to those people. People!" He shook his head, then glanced at the picture of his daughters on the wall before he sat down again.

"I know how you must feel, Derek, all your friends—"

"No, I never saw them before the day it happened."

"I didn't realize that. Then tell me again how it happened. How were the other kids involved?"

"Well, it was raining, and we were all at the bus stop out on Payne Road. This gray van was just going by very slowly, and I stopped it to get a ride for myself and this girl I'd seen. That's Pam. I saw her coming out of the lecture hall, and I really liked her. Then the other kids piled in, because they were all getting wet too. It just seemed like a lark. It was dark in the back of the van, but we were all laughing and kidding around. Afterward we figured out that they—the kidnappers—had been watching me."

"Describe the van again, Derek."

"Square. A GM van. Gray. There was a step on the passenger side. It locked in back, and there was a sliding door to the cab that locked, too. Four bolt holes on one side, as if a sign or something might have been bolted to it once. And they'd disconnected the lights. Just bare inside, no benches or anything."

"Do you remember the license number?"

"No," I said, but I shut my eyes and concentrated on that afternoon. The rain . . . running for the van with Pam . . . feeling so triumphant . . . that pretty, interesting girl was getting in with me! "There was an S on the plate," I said slowly. "And the first two numbers were—eight, yes, eight and five, and maybe the next number was three. I'm almost sure it was. Three."

"Good." Lieutenant Gordon was scribbling everything down. "They left Edward Hill in that van, is that right?"

"Yes. In the auto-wrecking yard."

"Go on. What else do you remember about the wrecking yard?"

"Well, it was night, I didn't see too much, but we heard Bogie open a gate before he drove in. Then we drove all the way down to the bottom of a hill, and there was a swamp. I smelled it. He left Ed there just before they went to pick up the money. That's when they locked me in the trunk of the car."

He nodded, looking down at the paper. "Your father reports that the woman contacted him again on Wednesday night about nine thirty-five—"

"That was after they shot Jeff and Wendy—"

"—and then again at twelve five. That would be when they had left Edward in the van and you were in the trunk. At four ten A.M. your father deposited the money at the Indian River rest stop, and at four twenty-two he phoned police headquarters."

Lieutenant Gordon picked up the phone. "Start searching the auto-wrecking yards for a gray GM van, license plate number S dash eight five three. It'll be near a swamp inside the wrecking yard. There's a boy, Edward Hill, locked inside."

He hung up. "Now let's go to the fire tower. Was there a sign at the beginning of the trail?"

"I think so. Just a wooden arrow."

"What did it say?"

I shook my head. "I've been trying to remember. They'd just shot Pam. I was—we were all in a state of shock."

"I understand. Try to think. Was there anything written on that arrow?"

I closed my eyes and tried to bring it back. All I could remember was being driven up the trail. "No, I can't remember." It upset me that I couldn't remember. "There was a sign. The trail was straight up a pretty steep hill. We crossed a stream, then we came to this big rock. It was about half a mile. They shot Wendy and Jeff in those woods, but not at the tower. Nearer the road."

"What was the road like? Was it paved, a lot of traffic?"

"No, no traffic, a dirt road."

"All right, now tell me again about where they shot

Pam. What kind of road was that? Do you remember anything? Road signs? Buildings? Anything?"

I shook my head despairingly. "I didn't see anything! I was in the van. It wasn't a highway. They went off the paved road. It was quiet, very isolated. It happened so fast."

"Okay, that all helps. Now, how long do you estimate they drove from the first place they kept you—"

"The lodge—"

"Yes, from there to the place they shot Pam?"

"The sun was coming up, just coming up when they shot her. It was dark, it was night when we left the boathouse. Maybe three hours? We were in so much darkness, my whole time sense was twisted."

"Any idea which way they drove? Direction? Uphill? On the highway? Or back roads? Did they turn a lot?"

I stared at him. All these questions. What good were they? For all I knew, they had driven in circles for three hours. Pam was out there on the ground somewhere. And we were sitting here talking. I jumped up, knocking over my chair.

"We have to go! Jeff and Wendy—Pam—don't you understand anything?" It was almost more than I could bear. "Stop talking and find them!"

A man looked through the glass wall. He was narrow-shouldered, sharp-faced. He stared at me. My throat spasmed. That menacing look, those cold eyes —was he another one? Another Bogie? He looked from me to the Lieutenant, then raised his hand and walked on.

Derek, you fool. It's over.

I leaned against Lieutenant Gordon's desk.

It was over for me. But not for Pam. Not for Ed, Wendy, Jeff. "I'm sorry I yelled."

"Listen, no sweat. I understand. I think we have enough now. We'll talk again. You get a rest. I'm ordering a helicopter to fly over the entire area and check the fire towers. I'll get someone to talk to some of the Forestry School boys and see if they can pinpoint the tower from your description. If we can locate the right one, we'll go in on the ground. But try to be patient. These things take time."

He'd left out Pam. He'd thought about Ed, Wendy, and Jeff. "Pam," I said. "What are you doing to find Pam?" *Never leave out Pam . . . You don't leave out Pam. Whatever happens, you don't leave out Pam.*

I thought he threw me a pitying glance. "We're going to look for the Barbushek girl, of course, but at this point we have almost nothing to go on."

Dad and I took a taxi back to the Washington Inn. I was exhausted. Dad ordered food from room service: fruit, rolls, and a quart of milk. "I called your mother while you were talking to Lieutenant Gordon," he said. "I promised her you'd call as soon as you could."

I lay down on the couch and took the phone. I talked to Mom, mainly reassuring her that I was all right. Then Ora got on the phone, and I talked some more. They were both flying in the next day. I don't even remember hanging up.

When I woke it was after dark. I was still on the couch. Dad had thrown a blanket over me. I must have slept for hours. My face—all my cuts and bruises ached. Dad had the papers, and I glanced at them while I drank some juice. The kidnapping story was on the front page of every paper, including *The New York Times*. The *Albany News Times* had our five pictures across the top of the page. Smiling school pictures. The one of Ed must have been taken in elementary school.

"Dad, did you see these pictures?"

He had business papers spread out on the desk. He took the newspaper, studied the pictures, then handed it back to me. "I'm sorry for those parents," he said. "Derek, remember when you talked to me on the phone? You said, 'Dad, there are five—' I thought you were telling me there were five kidnappers in the gang."

I studied the pictures again. Pam smiled out at me full face.

Later, I stood under the shower for a long time, letting the hot water soak into my body. I left the door open. I was waiting for the phone to ring. Lieutenant Gordon had said he'd get in touch the moment he had any news. I went over everything I'd told him. Had I forgotten anything that would help them find Pam? I was trying to fill in all the gaps. "Dad," I called, sticking my head out, "why didn't you show up Tuesday, when they were expecting you?"

"I had to get all that money in small bills without arousing anybody's suspicion, Derek. That's not easy. Those people set up an impossible situation. I needed another day."

I turned off the shower and took a towel. The boathouse had been burning when they came back that time. "You know, Dad, it was a good thing you didn't show up that first—" I cut myself off. What difference had it made to Pam, to Wendy, to Jeff?

I didn't think I'd sleep that night, but the moment I lay down I was out.

When I woke up, it was dark. I was in the attic. Ropes bound my wrists. I felt them cutting into my skin. I groaned. I felt the gag in my mouth.

"Derek?" The door to the connecting room opened. Light fell across the bed. I saw my father standing there, a pen in his hand. "Are you all right?"

"Just a dream." I got up and stumbled to the bathroom. I turned on the light and stood in front of the mirror, looking at myself. A bony bruised face, dark hair falling over my forehead. That's Derek Chapman, I told myself. Derek Chapman, you're free. I was trying to connect myself to myself, myself to this new world. Everything was still so strange. I was free, but in the depths of my being I was still a prisoner.

Suddenly I did a strange thing! I lowered my head and butted straight into the wall.

Why was I safe and not the others?

I butted my head again.

Please. Let them be all right. You. Whoever you are. Whatever you are. Let them be found safe.

I went back to bed. The next time I woke, it was daylight. Sun poured through half-closed blinds. The phone sat silently next to the bed. I'd been free for twenty-four hours, and still there was no word of the others.

20

Friday morning, after Dad and I had breakfast, I called all the parents of the other kids. I spoke to Mrs. Hill, both of Jeff's parents, Mr. Barbushek, and Wendy's father. It was an ordeal, because I couldn't give any of them, except Mrs. Hill, any real hope, but I kept calling until I'd spoken to everyone. Talking to Pam's father was the hardest of all. I was really destroyed when I got off the phone.

Later that day I went up in the helicopter with Lieutenant Gordon and a forest ranger, who sat with an aerial map in his lap and pinpointed every fire tower within a fifty-mile radius of the lodge where we'd been imprisoned. It had been found when someone in a neighboring township reported the boathouse fire. Now the lodge, which was located on Fowler Lake, had become the locus of the search.

I sat between the forest ranger and Lieutenant Gordon, a pair of binoculars glued to my eyes. There was so much land, so many lakes, streams, and threadlike roads going every way. *How will we ever find you, Pam?* We flew for hours, and saw nothing.

That night Dad and I met Mom and Ora at the airport. I was upset and emotional all over again. We went out for dinner together at the Highbridge Inn. It was the first time we'd all been together in eight years. I tried to be good company, but all I was really thinking about was tomorrow. Maybe we'd spot the fire tower, and then everything would fall into place. Jeff and Wendy would be found, we'd retrace our steps and find Pam. When I thought of it, I couldn't imagine their bodies. I kept imagining Jeff. Wendy. Pam. Each of them alive, laughing or talking. *Surprise, Derek! Fooled ya! Here we are!* And then I'd have to wrench myself back to reality.

My parents were talking about where they were going to send me to school for the remainder of the term. They agreed that I couldn't go back to Payne. I said yes to everything, but I knew that I wasn't leaving. Not yet, not till Pam and the others were found.

Saturday morning, I was still in bed when the phone rang. Dad picked it up. "Hello!" he barked. Since the day before, we'd been getting all kinds of nutty phone calls. It was really incredible: people asking for money, girls wanting me to go out with them, hate calls labeling me everything from a pinko commie to a capitalist-pig fascist. Then there were the creeps who threatened—or promised—to kidnap me again, and do it right this time.

Another kook call? Dad listened, one hand raised. "What is it, Dad?"

He put down the phone. "They found them."

"Pam," I breathed. And I started to shake.

"Derek—Derek! It's the boy and the girl. Wendy and Jeff. They found them. They're both in the hospital."

"Alive?"

"Yes!"

"Alive! Dad, they're *alive!*" I started pulling my clothes on over my pajamas. I didn't know what I was doing, I was so wild with relief and joy.

I went straight to the hospital. An early-morning commuter had found Jeff and Wendy wandering along a paved road. She'd driven them into Schenectady and straight to the hospital. Jeff was in the eye wing of Ellis Hospital, and Wendy was in a private room on the second floor. I went to see her first.

She was in bed, both her feet bandaged, white covers drawn right up to her chin. "Wendy, hello!" I put down the bunch of daffodils I'd brought and kissed her.

There was the same look on her face that she'd had when she sat on the window ledge of the tower, so pale and serious. She pushed herself up in the bed.

"Are you supposed to do that?" She looked as if a good gust of wind would blow her away.

"Oh, Derek, it's so good to see you."

She told me how she had followed us through the woods, leading Jeff, then stoned the van, hoping to put it out of commission. When Bogie started shooting, they'd run back into the woods. Neither of them had been hit. The darkness had saved them, but they had completely lost their bearings and gone even deeper into the woods.

"We wandered around for hours that night until we realized how lost we were. Three nights and two days, Derek."

"Did you have anything to eat?"

"Nothing. But we found a stream to drink from. That was so good. We thought if we followed it we'd find the path again, but we never did."

"Where'd you sleep at night?"

"We didn't! That first night, what was left of it, we crawled under a rock ledge. Only neither of us could close an eye, because we kept hearing noises. We were afraid it was Bogie. The next day I tried to move us in a straight line. But I guess I didn't do so good."

I looked down at her feet, huge now in the bandages.

"Remember? I left my sneakers at the tower, one inside, one outside. My feet, that's the worst part of me now. They got blistered and swollen and frostbitten. Jeff gave me his shoes, but his feet are so big that it only made the blisters worse. Derek—" She grabbed my hand. "Any news about Ed and Pam?"

"Nothing yet."

Her eyes filled with tears. "Jeff was so brave. We were all brave, weren't we, Derek?"

Later, I found Jeff on the fifth floor. He was in bed too, wearing a red silk Chinese robe. Both eyes were bandaged. "Who's there?" he said the moment I appeared. "That you again, Mom?"

I went to his side. "Jeff, it's me, Derek."

"Hey!" He put up his hand and gave me the brothers' handshake. Then we just clasped each other's hands for a moment.

His face was drawn. "I lost weight," he said. "My girl's not complaining about that. She said I was getting too fat anyway."

"Your eyes," I said. "Are they going to be okay?"

"I'm waiting for the word. The learned doctors were here a little while ago shining their lights in my eyes. The word so far is restrained optimism. They expect me to see again, but with some loss. Twenty percent. Thirty percent. It's all the same to them. It's not their eyes. But I am getting better," he said quickly. "They don't hurt the way they did before, and when they take off the bandages I see a little."

He wanted to know what had happened to me and Ed, and if they'd found Pam. Then he asked about Bogie and Pearl. I told him she was in a coma and he was in critical condition.

"Good," he said. "I hope they both die and go straight to hell!"

That was Saturday.

Sunday, the van was located and Ed was brought

into the hospital. He was badly dehydrated and in poor psychological condition. For eighty-four hours he'd been alone, bound and helpless, without food or water, not knowing if anybody would ever find him. Seeing him was a shock. It was his eyes. They were dark, sunken, glazed.

His mother was with him. She was in and out, calling the nurses for everything. She didn't want me to stay long. "Don't get him excited," she told me. "He's very nervous."

When I told Ed about seeing Wendy and Jeff, he sat up. "What did Wendy say about me?"

"You were the first one she asked about."

He nodded. "Tell her I'm coming to her room to see her tomorrow."

"Not tomorrow, Eddie," Mrs. Hill said. "Not till the doctor says you can get out of bed."

"I want to see her, Mom."

"Eddie—"

"Leave me alone, Mom, leave me alone!"

"All right, all right, don't get upset. Be calm, you've got to be calm." She turned to me. "You better go now," she said. "You've caused enough trouble already."

For a moment her words really hit me hard, made me feel punky and guilty. I looked away, looked down, started to mumble an apology. Then I caught myself. I couldn't go slinking through life because of my father's money.

"I'll see you, Ed," I said, grabbing one of his feet

and sort of shaking hands with it. "I'll be back tomorrow."

That night my family was together again for a few hours in Dad's suite. While Dad waited for a business call from Washington, we talked about what we could do to help the others. Dad was going to take care of all the medical bills, but he wanted to do something else. It was my mother's idea that he set up a trust fund for each of the kids, for their education. Dad said he'd get his lawyers to work on it right away.

"What about Lydia?" I said.

"The farm girl?" Dad said. "You're right. I'll have someone look into that, too."

Monday morning, I went out again with Lieutenant Gordon in a police cruiser. We drove around the area where Wendy and Jeff had been picked up. We located the fire tower; then we crisscrossed back and forth, going off the main road a hundred times to follow dirt roads, looking for the spot where they'd left Pam. I didn't know what else to look for except her body. But we didn't find anything.

Pearl died on Tuesday. By then they had found out that her real name was Sally Miles. She was only twenty-two and came from a small town in Indiana. She'd been a psychology major at the U. of Chicago, but had dropped out at the beginning of her third year. The TV ran a student picture of her wearing wire-rimmed glasses, with her hair pulled back in a pony tail.

Bogie was still on the critical list, but the police had talked to him. He had only one story. He didn't know anything about Pam's being shot. He didn't know anything about a road where they'd left her. He didn't know about shooting anybody. It was all so stupid, because he was going to stand trial and be convicted no matter what he did or didn't say. Kidnapping was a federal offense. There was no way in the world he could get around that.

His real name was Frederick Hartmann. He was twenty-six. His father was a machinist, and he had two brothers, one in the chemical business, the other a doctor. He had been in trouble all his life, a long list of offenses: assault, burglary, car theft.

Twenty-two and twenty-six. I'd thought they were a lot older. It was hard for me to believe they were ever young. Even when they were sixteen, they must have been ghouls.

That night, as I pulled the covers over my head and closed my eyes, I saw Pam's face. My mind replayed in detail the night we'd talked in the attic, and then the kiss we had shared. *Pam* . . . Tears filled my eyes. Before, I'd rarely cried. Now it seemed I was always emotional, often on the verge of tears. I thought that from now on my life would always be divided into before and after. Before the kidnapping and after. Before Pam was shot and after.

Wednesday morning it was raining. It was gray, depressing, like the day we'd been kidnapped. I'd never see a rainy day again without thinking of that

Saturday. Was it only eleven days ago? I wandered
back and forth through the suite until Dad asked me
to settle down or go out. He had work to do. For my
sake he was conducting business from the suite. He
was impatient to get back to New York, but he'd
agreed to stay in Schenectady with me till we had
word about Pam.

Later, I called Lieutenant Gordon's number. I got
the police switchboard. Lieutenant Gordon had
stepped out for a few minutes. What did I want?

"This is Derek Chapman. Is there anything new on
the kidnapping? Any word about Pam Barbushek?"

The policewoman on the switchboard said to wait
a minute while she checked around. She came back a
moment later and gave me the official brushoff: "The
investigation is continuing. There's nothing new to
report at this time." I banged down the phone.

"What's going on, Derek?" Dad asked.

"Those stupid bureaucrats! What are they doing?
They haven't done anything! Why haven't they found
her yet?"

The phone rang. "Chapman here," Dad said, pick-
ing up the receiver.

I went into the other room and started slamming a
pillow against the wall. *Pam* . . . SLAM . . . *Pam* . . .
SLAM . . . *Pam* . . .

"Derek, it's for you. Lieutenant Gordon wants to
talk to you."

"Hello," I said. "What is it?"

"Derek, Pam's been brought in."

I felt the breath go out of me. My eyes unfocused. I think I started to black out.

"An old man, a hermit from around Bog Lake, found her."

"Is she—is she—is she—" I couldn't say it. I didn't dare speak. I felt as if I were balanced on a tightrope. If I uttered the smallest sound . . . moved . . . even breathed . . . everything would fall apart.

"She's been shot twice. Once in the leg and once in the chest. Derek, are you there? I called her father first, then I called you."

Mutely I handed Dad the phone. I couldn't take it anymore. I slumped down in a chair.

Dad turned to me. "Derek, she's alive. Your friend is alive. She's been badly hurt, but she's alive."

I bent over, burying my face in my hands.

It was late that evening before they let me see Pam. By then I knew her story. A week before, the old man, a hermit, had been out digging leeks at dusk and found Pam crawling in the woods. He'd taken her back to his shack and cared for her. She'd been delirious for days. He had no phone, no electricity. For nearly thirty years he had lived alone. When he thought he could leave her, he walked eight miles to his nearest neighbor and asked the woman to call the hospital and tell them to send a doctor. A helicopter had flown in a doctor and two medics, and they had taken Pam out.

I saw her in the intensive-care room after an operation to remove the bullets. I stood next to the high white bed. She was swathed in bandages. I didn't recognize her. Was that small wizened person really Pam? It terrified me. There were so many tubes and bottles—a tube in her nose, another in the back of her hand. I stood there, afraid to even touch the bed, she looked so fragile.

Once her eyes opened. She stared up at me, but she didn't recognize me.

The next day the publicity over the kidnapping swelled to huge proportions. The newspapers loved the old man who had found Pam, and they dubbed him "The Hermit of the North Woods." CBS flew a team out to Bog Lake and got pictures and an interview with him for the evening news. All the papers carried stories about the kidnapping, with stuff about the old man and the same old things about me and my parents. And the kook calls started again, so bad that Dad started talking about hiring bodyguards for me and Ora. I hated the idea, and so did Ora.

One thing was clear to everyone: I wasn't going back to Payne School. Where would I go? We considered various schools, but, as Mom said, let just one reporter in one small town glom onto my being Derek Chapman and all the nuts would come crawling out of the woodwork again.

Mom thought of the Harleys. Maxwell Harley was a banker, a business friend of Dad's, and Mrs. Harley had gone to college with Mom. The Harleys had lived in Paris for ten years. Their three kids had all gone to the American School there and were in the

States now for college—which meant that there was plenty of room in their Paris apartment. Dad gave me the impression, too, that Mr. Harley owed him plenty of favors. He cabled him, asking if I could live with them the rest of the school year. Mr. Harley cabled back the next day that it was fine with both of them.

It happened so fast. "It's the best solution," Mom said when I started to balk. "You can be yourself there. Parisians just aren't all that interested in Americans." With that settled, Mom and Ora flew back to California.

Just a week after Pam was brought in, I saw her for the last time. Whenever I'd come into the hospital to see her in the preceding days there were always other people around—her father, other relatives, once a whole covey of doctors at the foot of her bed. And all the time she was weak, drugged against the pain. There were going to be several operations needed on her leg to repair her shattered kneecap, but first the doctors wanted to build up her strength.

Each time I went to see her, I found myself staring desperately at the vases of flowers, at the get-well cards lined up on the bureau, at the floor or out the window. Pam lay in the bed, her eyes heavy, sometimes sipping water through a bent straw, or lifting herself up for a moment to keep her lungs clear, her lips pressed tightly together.

In my mind I was always strong and reassuring. I'd be saying things that would bring us close again.

But in fact I never managed anything except the most banal chit chat. How are you? Did you sleep okay? How's the food?

That last day, as I went down the hall to her room, I heard someone crying. I thought it was Pam. I didn't want to go in. I waited for a moment, then pushed open the door. She was sleeping. Her hair was loose on the pillow. Her right leg was trussed up in some kind of contraption. The chest wound was already healing, but the doctors had told Dad they didn't know if her knee would ever function properly again.

I stood by the side of her bed, looking down at her. Her eyes opened. I put down my flight bag. "Dad's waiting for me. I'm going to the airport now." She nodded.

"We'll keep in touch," I said. "My whereabouts are a big military secret. All the mail has to go through Dad's New York office." She didn't say anything.

"My parents' idea."

Her lips were so pale.

I moved closer to her.

Say something, Pam. Remember that night we kissed. I'll never forget it.

Her eyes closed. Opened. Closed again. Tears slipped from the corners. ". . . Never walk again," she whispered.

I was choking. "Pam—Pam—"

Her eyes opened. She looked at me bitterly. "Go away, Derek."

21

Those next months, living in Paris with the Harleys, were very strange. Paris—it should have been a fantastic time for me. Paris is a beautiful city; everything everyone has ever said about it is true. I'd been there before, briefly, but never lived there. It took me one day of getting lost on the Metro, but after that I knew my way around. I went everywhere, alone. I *was* alone. The Harleys had a busy social life. Most of the time when I came back from school and in the evenings only Mme. Goncourt, the maid, was in the apartment. She was a French woman; she rarely said anything to me, and then only in French. Even though I didn't see much of Mr. and Mrs. Harley, I think they were keeping watch over me through Mme. Goncourt. A couple of times when I went out I was sure I saw her.

I went to school, kept up with my work, wrote my mother, and called Dad's office once a week (as per our agreement), assuring everyone that I was safe and not being bothered. But all the time there was a part of me holding back, keeping a distance, a curtain maybe, between me and the world.

I did a lot of reading in those months, and a lot of thinking. Something terribly important had happened to me, and now no one wanted to talk about it. "Just try to forget it," my mother wrote me, and over the phone my father gave me similar advice: "The less said the better."

But I couldn't put those days of the kidnapping out of my mind. What had happened to me, to the others, had to have some meaning. We couldn't live through something like that and then just dismiss it. Those six days had been so awful, so intense, that what had happened then seemed realer to me still than what was happening to me now. The relationships, the emotions, the feelings, the life-or-death level at which every moment had been lived still remained with me. It was a crazy thing to think, but I sometimes felt that I was more alive then, in the forests and mountains around Schenectady, New York, than I was now in Paris, France.

How could all that just disappear? In school sometimes I'd hear my name called out in class—"Derek Chapman"—and I'd be caught totally by surprise. *Derek Chapman.* What did it mean to be Derek Chapman? Why was I here? Why in Paris? Why living with the Harleys? It was a time of intense confusion, of brooding, of thinking. A time of loneliness, a time of waiting.

Every few weeks Dad's secretary sent me a brisk

note letting me know what was going on with Pam and Jeff.

Dear Derek,

Jeff is out of the hospital. He continues to go to Dr. Garcia for checkups. His vision has been stabilized with a 15% loss due to scar tissue. He doesn't need glasses now, but may in the future.

Wendy's feet are completely healed. She has to be careful in the future that she doesn't expose them to extreme cold, but Dr. Lockwood sees no reason for her not to go on with all her usual activities.

Pam's knee was operated on for the second time by Doctors Fellows and Gold. Her leg is in a cast. She is at home, being tutored, and doesn't experience undue discomfort. I will let you know any further developments.

> *Best,*
>
> *Marcia*

Dear Derek,

Pam's cast was removed. The operation was a success but she is still unable to walk unaided. She has been equipped with a wheelchair.

> *Best,*
>
> *Marcia*

Wendy was writing me too, sending the mail care of Dad's New York office, which forwarded it to me.

She had appointed herself sort of official letter-writer and keeper-in-touch for the five of us. I saved all of Wendy's letters, and read them often enough to know them almost by heart. Sometimes I felt closer to Wendy, Ed, Jeff, and Pam than to my own family. I could see each of them in my mind in complete detail, hear their voices, remember how they laughed, and, eerily, even know what they'd say about things that were happening to me now.

It was Wendy who wrote me that Ed was having recurrent nightmares, which were so upsetting that he was going to a psychologist for help. Ed put a postscript on more than one of her letters, so I had an idea they were together a lot.

Jeff wrote me one long letter, after I'd written him about the Paris School of Mime, which I thought he'd be interested in. He agreed with me that we five ought to stay in touch, and wrote about his negotiations for a summer-theater job. The last thing he mentioned was about Pam. He and his girlfriend, Arletta, had gone to visit her. "She's coming out of the shadows now."

I thought about that line a lot, tried to read into it what was really happening with Pam. In that whole period when I was in Europe she never wrote to me, and except for one transatlantic botch of a phone call I never tried to contact her.

In the middle of June, Marcia wrote me: "Pam will be spending three weeks at the Hoskins Orthopedic clinic in New York City, July 8 through July 29, for intensive physical therapy with Dr. Michael Rosen, the most highly regarded specialist in this area of medicine."

At the end of June, Ora finished school and went to a horse ranch in New Hampshire, and Mom flew over to Paris to visit for a few days before she and I drove to the villa she'd rented on the Mediterranean. On our very last day in Paris I called Pam.

"Pam? This is Derek Chapman. How are you?"

"Derek?"

"How are you? I mean—"

"I'm fine."

"You are?"

"Yes, sure."

"Your operation—"

"What did you say? I can't hear you too well. There's an awful lot of interference on this line."

"I said—Pam, listen—Pam, your leg, how is it?"

"I'm fine, Derek, just fine. Can you hear me? Where are you calling from, anyway?"

"I really can't say, Pam."

"What? This is an overseas call, isn't it? This must be costing you a fortune."

"It doesn't matter—" I tried desperately to read her tone of voice. Was she sarcastic? Bitter? Indifferent? Was she just waiting for me to hang up? What was she really thinking, feeling? I couldn't tell, and I didn't know how to ask. We ended up saying some stupid things about what a hot summer it was so far, and then we hung up.

The summer at Eze-sur-Mer passed slowly for me. I swam in the pool every day, read, went to a few parties Mom gave for friends, met some other kids about my age. The best thing was talking to Mom. Just this and that, nothing really, but we became closer.

Through Wendy I heard what the other kids were doing that summer. Jeff had gotten his job with a summer theater in Cape Cod, as a scenery painter and "go-for." Not exactly the lead part, but he was pleased. Wendy had a job, too, working as a mother's helper for a family with a summer cottage on Lake George. She had planned to pick out Cocoa Two from a litter of miniature French poodles when school ended, but decided to put it off till she returned from her summer job. Ed was on his aunt's dairy farm in central New York.

With Pam in New York City, it meant we were all in different places, worlds apart. I couldn't help wondering if I would ever see Pam again, and if I did, if we would be any more than two strangers who had shared a terrible experience.

Weeks before I got my parents' permission, I knew I wanted to go home to the United States. By the time they said okay, it was so late Dad had to pull strings to get me into a school. But he managed.

Ora's camp season was over the third week in August. My mother decided the three of us would spend a few days together in New York City; then she and Ora would go back to California, and I'd fly

down to Charleston and enter my school ten days
early. Dad was going to be in Japan on business, so
I probably wouldn't see him till sometime in the
winter.

When I said something to Mom about wanting to
visit the other kids in Schenectady, she got upset. She
was still nervous about me, and didn't want me anywhere near that area. I decided not to lock horns with
her, and let it drop.

It wasn't until I'd seen her and Ora off on their
plane to Los Angeles and I was sitting in the airport
lounge waiting for my own plane that I suddenly
decided to check out flights to Schenectady. I could
be there in an hour, and there was a flight out to
Charleston an hour and a half later. I went into a
phone booth and dialed Pam's number. I was calm. I
didn't expect her to answer. If she did, it would be a
sign.

Marcia had written that Pam's therapy had been
successful. She was home again, and was being
tutored so she could enter her senior year with her
class.

The phone rang. I counted. One . . . two . . . three
. . . It was crazy. She could be anywhere. Six . . .
seven . . . I let it ring. I'd stop at ten. Nine . . .

"Hello," Pam said.

"Pam?"

"Yes, who is this?"

"Pam, I—" My throat closed up.

"Derek? Is this Derek? Derek, is it you?"

In a rush, I blurted everything out—my coolness completely gone—asking her if she could come to the airport, if she *would* come because I would have only a little more than an hour between flights. Everything in one hurried sentence.

"All right," she said.

"What?"

"I'll meet you. I'll be there. Okay?"

"Yes. Good. Fine." I hung up, sweating, scared, relieved, happy, scared, God, how scared I was.

A few hours later I walked off the plane in Schenectady, out through the long movable corridor attached to the plane, then past the boarding areas, wondering if I'd recognize Pam. Telling myself not to be a fool. Scared again. Scared she wouldn't show up. Scared that if she did I'd be as mute, as tongue-tied, as I'd been when she was in the hospital.

Go away, Derek.

I'd never forget that.

Then I saw her, at the end of one of those long corridors, limping toward me. She was wearing jeans and a pink flowered shirt. Her hair was under a blue kerchief. She was wearing big silver hoops in her ears.

I walked faster. I raised my hand. She waved. She still walked with her head high, swinging her arms. I remembered the first time I'd seen her, how she walked ahead of everyone, but without seeming to hurry. Now people streamed past her.

"Hello, Derek." She was smiling. A beautiful, wonderful smile. She was smiling at me. I ran. We met and hugged. Then we stepped apart. Her face was flushed and full.

"How are you?" I said, articulate as ever.

"Fine."

I wanted to hug her again, but I didn't dare. "I mean, how are you really. Really?"

"Fine. I'm really fine, Derek. Listen, how much time do you have? Just an hour?"

"More. About an hour and a half."

"Shall we go somewhere and talk? Or what do you want to do?"

"Talk," I said. "Talk to you, that's great, that's all I want to do."

She led the way down the long windowed passageway and out into the terminal, then up a short flight of stairs to a small passenger lounge, where we found a couch in a dark corner and sat down next to each other. I started talking, telling her what had happened to me after she was shot, especially when Bogie had meant to kill me. I talked and talked. I hadn't known I was going to talk so much, say any of this. I told her about those days when she was missing, how afraid I was that she was dead, how I woke each morning dreading what I'd hear.

As I talked to her I became very agitated. It all came back to me as vividly as if it were happening now. My mouth dried out. It was hard for me to swallow. "When I heard you were alive, I thought it was a miracle. That any of us lived through all that. I've thought of nothing else for months. No one wants to talk about it anymore, but I can't stop thinking about it. It means something, it's terribly important— are you with me, Pam?"

"All the way."

"I haven't put it all together yet. Why we five? I know why me. But why Jeff? Why you? Are you bitter? I know you must be bitter. In the hospital when you said, 'Go away, Derek,' I understood. I tried to understand. You were bitter."

"Yes. I *was* bitter. I felt so bitter. Hateful. I'd never felt that way before. Not even after my mother died. This was worse. This terrible thing that had happened to me. Being crippled. I never hurt anyone! Why would anyone want to hurt me?" She gave me a long look, a Pam look, her eyes wide and brilliant.

"You know, Derek, when it was happening, after I was shot, I was conscious for hours. All the time till that old man found me. I knew I was badly hurt. And all I thought about then was surviving. I didn't want to die. I wanted to live, and I think I helped myself by wanting so much. I crawled away from the road— I was terrified they'd come back and shoot me again. I thought about hiding myself—"

"Yes," I said. "That feeling of being exposed."

She nodded. "I knew just what you meant when you said you felt that way after Bogie tried to kill you."

"Go on," I said.

"Well, I knew I needed water. I drank from a puddle. Like an animal, Derek, but I would have done anything to live. Afterward, though, that's when things got worse. The bitterness I felt! It was the most awful hell of all. It made everything a thousand times worse. It made my loneliness worse. It made the pain worse. Almost all summer I hated waking up in the morning. I didn't know if my leg would ever work right again. I was in a really deep depression. Then, as my body healed, my mind healed also." She pulled off her scarf and freed her hair.

"Derek, we're alive! That's what matters. Waking up in the morning. Seeing the sun. Or feeling rain on your face. Just breathing! I have never felt how beautiful life is till now. I want to live right. I want to do something good in the world. I never want anything to do with violence or pain for others. I want to let all the unimportant things slip away. Do you understand, Derek?" she said intensely.

"Yes."

"Really?"

"Yes. You said everything I feel. Everything."

"I knew you'd understand!"

A few minutes later, my flight was announced. We stood there talking. I hated to leave her. I wanted to kiss her.

"Derek." She touched my cheek. "We'll write each other." Then she kissed me.

I thought it was good-bye, but at the last minute she said she was coming to the boarding area with me. We walked down the corridor holding hands.

"You won't have any trouble getting a taxi home, will you?" I said.

"Taxi." She laughed. "My father's my taxi. He's waiting for me outside."

"He brought you here? That was nice of him."

"*Nice!* Ordinary people like us don't take taxis, Derek. It would have cost fifteen dollars to come here by cab. We haven't got that kind of money."

"I still don't know about money," I said. "Not really. Not the way you do, Pam. Even now, after everything that's happened to me!"

"Hey, don't be upset. It isn't that important. Being rich is just one of those miserable facts of life you have to live with—like my limp, maybe."

We stopped at the boarding area. I wanted to kiss her again, but the airline steward was standing right there, watching us. I shifted my flight bag from one shoulder to the other. "I hate good-byes."

"Me too. It always seems like there's so much to say and no time left—"

"Pam, I—"

"No, *go*." She gave me a little shove. "I really do hate good-byes!" She started to walk away, then turned. "Derek, think of me sometimes."

In the plane I found my seat next to the window. All the time we were taxiing I looked out the window, hoping to catch a glimpse of Pam. We climbed steeply above the city, everything receding, green fields, clusters of tiny white houses, a river, and roads like silver threads over the land, the world turning to a map beneath me.

Think of me sometimes. Pam's words had seemed

full of hope and promise, but now I heard the hesitation, the shadow of doubt. Chance had gathered us up in its net, flung us together. But now the net had emptied. The roar of the plane's accelerating engines seemed to match the turmoil inside me.

Pam . . . good-bye . . . *No*—just for now. Pam, do you hear me? We won't grow apart. We'll write, we'll see each other. I'll write you; I'll write you so often you won't be able to forget me.

I took pen and paper from my flight bag. "Dear Pam," I wrote, but then for a long time I just sat there looking out over the spreading horizon.

ABOUT THE AUTHORS

NORMA FOX MAZER has written seventeen books and is the author of *After the Rain*, a Newbery Honor book for 1988. HARRY MAZER, who has written thirteen books, is the author of *The Girl of His Dreams*, which was named a Best Book for Young Adults by the American Library Association. They teamed up for the second time in their careers with *Heartbeat*, a Bantam Starfire novel. The Mazers have four grown children and live near Syracuse, New York.